James Hadley Chase and The Murder Room

›› This title is part of The Murder Room, our series dedicated to making available out-of-print or hard-to-find titles by classic crime writers.

Crime fiction has always held up a mirror to society. The Victorians were fascinated by sensational murder and the emerging science of detection; now we are obsessed with the forensic detail of violent death. And no other genre has so captivated and enthralled readers.

Vast troves of classic crime writing have for a long time been unavailable to all but the most dedicated frequenters of second-hand bookshops. The advent of digital publishing means that we are now able to bring you the backlists of a huge range of titles by classic and contemporary crime writers, some of which have been out of print for decades.

From the genteel amateur private eyes of the Golden Age and the femmes fatales of pulp fiction, to the morally ambiguous hard-boiled detectives of mid twentieth-century America and their descendants who walk our twenty-first century streets, The Murder Room has it all. ››

The Murder Room
Where Criminal Minds Meet

themurderroom.com

James Hadley Chase (1906–1985)

Born René Brabazon Raymond in London, the son of a British colonel in the Indian Army, James Hadley Chase was educated at King's School in Rochester, Kent, and left home at the age of 18. He initially worked in book sales until, inspired by the rise of gangster culture during the Depression and by reading James M. Cain's *The Postman Always Rings Twice*, he wrote his first novel, *No Orchids for Miss Blandish*. Despite the American setting of many of his novels, Chase (like Peter Cheyney, another hugely successful British noir writer) never lived there, writing with the aid of maps and a slang dictionary. He had phenomenal success with the novel, which continued unabated throughout his entire career, spanning 45 years and nearly 90 novels. His work was published in dozens of languages and over thirty titles were adapted for film. He served in the RAF during World War II, where he also edited the RAF Journal. In 1956 he moved to France with his wife and son; they later moved to Switzerland, where Chase lived until his death in 1985.

No Orchids for Miss Blandish
Eve
More Deadly Than the Male
Mission to Venice
Mission to Siena
Not Safe to Be Free
Shock Treatment
Come Easy – Go Easy

What's Better Than Money?
Just Another Sucker
I Would Rather Stay Poor
A Coffin from Hong Kong
Tell it to the Birds
One Bright Summer Morning
The Soft Centre
You Have Yourself a Deal
Have This One on Me
Well Now, My Pretty
Believed Violent
An Ear to the Ground
The Whiff of Money
The Vulture Is a Patient Bird
Like a Hole in the Head
An Ace Up My Sleeve
Want to Stay Alive?
Just a Matter of Time
You're Dead Without Money
Have a Change of Scene
Knock, Knock! Who's There?
Goldfish Have No Hiding Place
So What Happens to Me?
The Joker in the Pack
Believe This, You'll Believe Anything
Do Me a Favour, Drop Dead
I Hold the Four Aces
My Laugh Comes Last
Consider Yourself Dead

You Must Be Kidding
A Can of Worms
Try This One for Size
You Can Say That Again
Hand Me a Fig Leaf
Have a Nice Night
We'll Share a Double Funeral
Not My Thing
Hit Them Where It Hurts

Just Another Sucker

James Hadley Chase

An Orion book

Copyright © Hervey Raymond 1961

The right of James Hadley Chase to be identified as the author of this
work has been asserted in accordance with the Copyright, Designs and
Patents Act 1988.

This edition published by
The Orion Publishing Group Ltd
Orion House
5 Upper St Martin's Lane
London WC2H 9EA

An Hachette UK company
A CIP catalogue record for this book is available from the British Library

ISBN 978 1 4719 0345 8

www.orionbooks.co.uk

CHAPTER ONE

WHEN they released me at eight o'clock on a July morning, it was raining fit to drown a duck.

It was a pretty odd sensation to walk out into the world that, for me, had stood still for three and a half long years. I approached it warily, walking a few yards from the iron studded doors, then pausing to get the feel of freedom.

There would be a Greyhound bus at the corner to take me home, but for the moment, I didn't feel like going home. I just wanted to stand on the edge of the sidewalk, to feel the rain against my face and to let the fact sink in that I was now free, that I wouldn't have to spend another night in a cell and I wouldn't any longer have to share my life with thugs, criminals and sex perverts as I had been doing for all these months.

The rain made puddles in the road. It beat down on my four year old hat and my five-year old raincoat: warm rain, coming from a cloud-swollen sky as dark and as bitter as myself.

A glittering Buick Century slid up beside me and the electrically driven off-side window rolled down.

'Harry!'

The car door swung open as I bent to stare in at the driver. John Renick grinned at me.

'Come on in — you're getting wet,' he said.

I hesitated, then I got into the car and slammed the door shut. Renick grabbed my hand and squeezed it. His dark lean face showed as nothing else could how pleased he was to see me.

'How are you, you old sonofagun?' he asked. 'How does it feel to be out?'

'I'm all right,' I said disentangling my hand from his. 'Don't tell me I'm getting a police escort back home.'

His smile slipped a little at my tone: his grey shrewd eyes searched my face.

1

'You didn't imagine I wasn't coming, did you? I've been counting the days.'

'I didn't imagine anything.' I looked at the ornate dashboard of the car. 'Is this yours?'

'You bet. I bought it a couple of months ago. She's a honey, isn't she?'

'So the Palm City cops are still keeping themselves well heeled. Congratulations.'

His mouth tightened and there was a sudden flash of anger in his eyes.

'Look, Harry, if any other guy but you had made that crack, I would have taken a poke at him.'

I shrugged.

'Go ahead if you feel that way. I'm used to cops taking pokes at me.'

He drew in a deep breath then he said: 'Just for the record, I'm the D.A.'s Special officer now, and I have had a pretty substantial rise. I've been off the regular Force for more than two years.'

I was irritated to feel the blood rise to my face.

'I see ... I'm sorry ... I didn't know.'

'How could you?' He grinned and shifted into gear.

The Buick drifted away from the kerb. 'A lot of things have changed, Harry, since you've been inside. The old gang has gone. We have a new D.A. — he's a good man.'

I didn't say anything.

'What are your plans?' he asked abruptly.

'I haven't any. I want to look around. You know the *Herald's* washed me up?'

'I heard.' There was a pause, then he went on: 'It's going to be a, little rough for you at first. You know that, don't you?'

'Oh sure. When a guy kills a cop even accidentally, he's not allowed to forget it. I know how rough it is going to be.'

'You won't have any trouble with the police. I didn't mean; that, but you may have, to look around for a new career. Cubitt carries a lot of weight. He has his knife in you. If he can stop you, you're not getting back into the newspaper world.'

'You let me worry about that.'

'I might be able to help.'

2

'I don't want any help?'

'Oh sure, but there's Nina...'

'And I can take care of Nina.'

There was a long pause while he stared-through the rain-soaked windshield, then he said: 'Look Harry, you and I are friends. We've known each other a heck of a long time. I know how you arc feeling, but don't treat me as if I were one of your enemies. I've talked to Meadows about you. He's the new, D.A. There's nothing fixed yet but there's a chance we can use you in the office.'

I looked at him.

'I wouldn't work for the Palm City Administration if it was the last job left on earth.'

'Nina's had a pretty rough time,' Renick said awkwardly. 'She...'

'I've also had a pretty rough time, so that makes the two of us. I don't want anyone's help. That's final!'

'Well, okay,' Renick said. He made a helpless gesture with his hands. 'Don't imagine I don't understand, Harry. I guess I'd be bitter too if I had been framed the way you were, but what's done's done. You have your future to think of now — Nina's future too.'

'What else do you imagine I have been thinking about all the time I have been in a cell?' I stared out of the car window at the sea, grey in the rain, pounding against the sea wall. 'Yes, I'm bitter all right. I have had time to realize just what a goddam sucker I've been. I should have taken the ten thousand dollars the Police Commissioner offered me to keep my mouth shut. Well, one thing I have learned since I have been in jail: I'm not ever going to be a sucker again.'

'You're just sounding off,' Renick said sharply. 'You know you did the right thing. The cards were stacked against you. If you had taken that rat's bribe, you would never have been able to live with yourself, and you know it.'

'Think so? Don't kid yourself it's going to be all that pleasant to live with myself now. Three and a half years sharing a cell with a child rapist and two thugs with habits that would sicken a pig does something to you. At least if I had taken that bribe I wouldn't be now an ex-jailbird without a job. I'd probably be owning a car like yours.

3

Renick shifted uneasily.

'That's no way to talk, Harry. You're getting me worried. For Pete's sake, get hold of yourself before you see Nina.'

'Suppose you mind your own business?' I snarled at him. 'Nina happens to be my wife. She's taken me for better or worse. Well, okay. You let me worry about her.'

'I think you were wrong, Harry, when you wouldn't let her attend the trial or even visit you in jail or write to you. You know as well as I do, she wanted to share this thing with you, but you turned her into an outsider.'

My hands closed into fists as I continued to stare at the rain-soaked beach.

"I knew what I was doing,' I said. 'Do you imagine I' wanted her to be photographed by those vultures in the court room? Do you imagine I wanted her to see me in that prison rig behind wire and glass? Do you imagine I wanted that jerk of a Warden reading her letters before I' got them? Just because I acted like a sucker, there was no need for her to be dragged into it.'

'You were wrong, Harry. Didn't it occur to you she wanted to be with you,' Renick said impatiently. 'It was as much as I could do to persuade her not to come with me this morning.'

We were approaching Palm Bay, the swank residential district of Palm City. The long line of de luxe bathing cabins looked forlorn in the driving rain. The beach was deserted. The Cadillacs, the Rolls and the Bentleys stood in their parking squares outside the luxury hotels.

At one time Palm Bay had been my hunting ground. It seemed a long time now since I had been the gossip columnist of the *Herald*, the newspaper with the biggest circulation in California. Then, my column had been syndicated to over a hundred minor newspapers. I had been earning good money. I had lived well an had enjoyed my work. After a while, I had married Nina and bought a bungalow just outside Palm Bay where we set up home. I was doing all right, and looked set for life-; then one night, when I was in the bar of the Beach Hotel, I happened to overhear a snatch of conversation between two strangers who had been hitting the bottle and had become indiscreetly loud.

Those few words put me on to something that was as hot and as dangerous as an exploding volcano. It took me two months of secret and patient investigation before I got the complete story. It was a story that would hit the headlines of the *Herald* for weeks.

A Chicago mob planned to take over Palm City. They planned to install slot machines, to set up brothels and all the rest of the paraphernalia of organized vice. The monthly take was estimated to be two and a half million dollars.

When I had convinced myself of the facts, I thought at first this mob must be crazy. I couldn't believe they could just walk in and take over this city how and when they liked. Then I got a hot tip that the Palm City Police Commissioner as well as half a dozen of the important administrators had been bought and had agreed to give the mob the protection it needed.

Then I made my major mistake: I tried to carry on the investigation on my own. I wanted this to be a personal scoop, and it wasn't until I had got the necessary evidence and an outline of the articles I intended to write exposing the conspiracy that I went to J. Matthew Cubitt, my boss and owner of the *Herald*.

I told him what was cooking and he listened, his grey, thin face expressionless.

When I was through, he said he would want to check my facts. There was a coldness in his manner and an odd lack of enthusiasm that should have warned me. Although I had dug deep and had persuaded a lot of people to talk, I hadn't dug deep enough. The mob had bought the *Herald*. That was something I had never thought possible. I learned later they had promised Cubitt a seat in the Senate if he played along with them and the bribe had been too much for this grasping, ambitious newspaper owner.

He asked me to turn over all my information to him to check. On my way back to the bungalow to get the dossier, I was stopped by a police car.

The Police Commissioner, I was told, wanted to see me. I was escorted to police headquarters where I had an interview with the Commissioner.

He was a hard, direct man and he didn't attempt to

5

hedge. He put on his desk ten thousand dollars in new crisp bills. He would trade the bills for the dossier and I could forget the investigation. How about it?

Apart from the fact I had never taken a bribe and didn't intend to start now, I knew the story I was ready to write would put my name on the front page for weeks and would establish my reputation in the newspaper world as nothing else could. I got up and walked out, and I walked right into trouble.

I turned my dossier over to Cubitt and told him of the bribe offered me by the Police Commissioner. He stared at me with his hooded eyes, nodded and told me to come to his house at half past ten that night. By then I would have had time to check on my findings and decide the best way to handle the set-up. I guessed he burned the dossier. I never saw it again.

Nina had been in on the investigation from the start. She was scared sick about it, realizing as I did, the kind of dynamite I was handling but she also realized this was my big chance and she went along with me.

I left home just before ten for my date with Cubitt. I could see how scared she was as she went with me to the car. I had an uneasy feeling myself, but I trusted Cubitt.

His residence was in Palm Bay. To get there, I had to drive along a stretch of lonely road. On this road, I ran into trouble.

A police car, travelling fast, overtook me and sideswiped me. The idea maybe was to force my car off the road and into the sea, but it didn't work out that way. There was a pretty bad smash and the police driver got his ribs shoved in by his steering wheel. His companion, apart from a shaking, wasn't hurt. He arrested me for dangerous driving. I knew it was a frame-up, but there was nothing I could do about it. A couple of minutes later, another police car arrived with Sergeant Bayliss of the Homicide Squad at the wheel. What he was doing on this lonely road no one ever bothered to ask. He took charge. The injured cop was rushed to hospital and I was taken to headquarters.

On the way, Bayliss suddenly told the driver to stop. We were in a dark, deserted street. He told me to get out. The driver got out too and grabbed me from behind, locking my arms. Bayliss took a bottle of Scotch from the glove compartment, filled his mouth with whisky and sprayed the whisky in my face and over my, shirt. Then he produced a blackjack and clubbed me over the head.

I came to in a cell, and from that moment, I was sunk. The injured cop died. They nailed me on a manslaughter rap and I drew four years. The attorney who defended me fought like a tiger, but he didn't get anywhere. When he introduced the conspiracy evidence, it was promptly thrown out. Cubitt, on oath, said he never had my dossier, and that he was going to get rid of me anyway as I was not only an unreliable newspaper man, but a secret drunk.

All the time I was serving my sentence I kept thinking what a sucker I had been. I told myself I must have been crazy to have tried to buck the Administration on my own.

It didn't help me when I heard the Police Commissioner had resigned under pressure, and that the Administration had had a complete shake up. There had been an inquiry after the hints my attorney had dropped around and the Chicago mob had decided to move in elsewhere, but that didn't help me. I was stuck with a four years sentence for killing a cop while drunk in charge of a car, and there was nothing anyone could do about it.

And now, after spending three and a half years in a cell, I was free again, I was a newspaper man with no other training. Cubitt had blacklisted me, and that meant I wouldn't get any other newspaper work. I would have to make a new career for myself I had no idea what I was going to do. Although I earned well, I had always been a spender. I hadn't left Nina much to live on when I went to jail. There wouldn't be much left now: if anything. I had worried myself sick wondering what she was doing and what was happening to her, but I was obstinate and stupid enough to insist through my attorney that she shouldn't write to me. The thought of that fat, sadistic Warden reading her letters before I got them was something I just couldn't take.

I said to Renick, 'How has she been making out? How is she?'

'She's fine,' he told me. 'You didn't doubt that, did you? She's discovered a talent for art. She decorates pottery of all things and makes quite a good living out of it.'

He swung the Buick around the corner of the street in which I had my home.

The sight of the bungalow brought a lump to my throat. The familiar street was deserted. The rain came down in grey sheets, bouncing on the, road and the sidewalk.

Renick pulled up outside the front gate.

'I'll be seeing you,' he said and gripped my arm. 'You're lucky, Harry. I wish I had someone like Nina waiting for me.'

I got out of the car. Without looking at him, I started up the familiar path. Then the front door swung open, and there was Nina.

II

Around six-thirty on the seventh morning after my release from jail, I came awake abruptly. I had been dreaming I was back in a cell, and it took me a moment or so to realize I was in my own bedroom with Nina sleeping at, my side.

I lay on my back and stared up at the ceiling and began to wonder, as I had been wondering for the past seven days what I was going to do to earn a living. I had already probed the newspaper world. As I had expected, there was nothing for me. Cubitt's influence spread like the tentacles of an octopus. Even the minor local paper was afraid to touch me.

There wasn't much else I could do. Writing was my profession, but I wasn't a creative writer. I was a reporter. I had to have facts before I could produce good copy. Without the facilities of a newspaper behind me I was sunk.

I looked at Nina, sleeping by my side.

I had married her two years and three months before I went to jail. Then she had been twenty-two and I had been twenty-seven.

She had dark wavy hair and her skin was the colour of ivory. We both had agreed she wasn't beautiful in the accepted sense of the word, but I had declared, and still thought so, that she was the most attractive woman I had ever seen. Watching her, as she slept, I could see how much she had suffered. The skin around her eyes was too tight. There was a droop to her lips that hadn't been there when I had left her to serve my

8

sentence and she looked sad: a thing she had never looked when asleep in the old days.

She had had a rough time all right. I had left her three thousand dollars in our joint account, but this had gone quickly: my attorney's fee and the last payment on the bungalow had taken most of it, and she had had to look for work.

She had had several jobs, then finally, as Renick had told me, she had discovered a talent for art and had got a job with a man who sold pottery to the tourists. He made the pots and she decorated them. She had been earning sixty dollars a week for the past year: enough as she explained to me, to keep us going until I could take over again.

I now had only two hundred dollars left in my account. When that was gone, and unless I found a job, I would have to ask her for bus fares, money for cigarettes, and so on: the thought of having to do that demoralized me.

The previous day, growing desperate, I had tried to find a temporary job — anything that would bring me in a little money.

After tramping around most of the day, I came home still empty handed. I was too well known in Palm City to be offered a menial job. The guys who wanted a man were embarrassed when they saw me.

'Aw, Mr. Barber, you're kidding,' they said to me. 'This is no job for you.'

I hadn't the guts to tell them how flat broke I was, and they were relieved when I made a joke and left.

'What are you thinking about, Harry?' Nina asked, rolling over on her side to look at me.

'Nothing... I was dozing.'

'You're worrying, but you mustn't. We'll make out. We can get along fine on sixty a week. We're not going to starve. You must be patient. The right job will come along.'

'And while I'm waiting for the right job to come along, I will have to live on you,' I said. 'Well that's wonderful. I'll enjoy it.'

She lifted her head to stare at me. Her dark eyes anxious.

'We're partners, Harry. When you get a job, I'll retire. As you haven't a job for the moment, then I do the work. That's the way a partnership should be.'

9

'Thanks for telling me.'

'Harry... you're worrying me. You may not realize it, but you have changed so much. You're so hard and bitter now. You must try to forget. We have our lives to lead together, and this attitude of yours...'

'I know.' I got out of bed. 'I'm sorry about it. Maybe if you had spent three and a half years in jail, you might feel the same way as I do. I'll fix the coffee. At least, that's something I can do these days.'

All this that I'm telling you about happened two years ago. Looking back on it, and taking it now in its right perspective, I realize I was a pretty weak kind of character. I can see I had let this frame-up and the prison sentence get on top of me. I wasn't tough and bitter. I was eaten up with self-pity.

If I had had what it takes, I would have got rid of the bungalow, and with Nina, I would have gone some place where I wasn't known and made a new career for myself. Instead I went around looking for a job that didn't exist for me in this town and making a martyr of myself.

For the next ten days I went around pretending to look for the non-existent job. I made out to Nina that I was hunting all day, but it was a lie. After making a couple of calls and being turned down I sought sanctuary in the nearest bar.

When I had worked as a columnist, I had never been much of a drinker, but now, I began really to hit the bottle. Whisky was the one magic escape for me. With five or six whiskies inside me, nothing seemed to matter. I didn't give a damn if I had a job or not, I could return home and watch Nina slave at her art work without feeling like a pimp.

With a load on, I even found it was easy to lie to her.

'I was talking to a guy this morning, and it looks as if we can make a deal,' I told her. 'He wants me to write a series of articles around his hotel, but first he has to talk to his partner. If it jells, it'll pay over three hundred a week.'

There was no guy, no partner and no hotel, but the lie kept me important, and it was essential to my ego that Nina should still think I was important. Even when I was forced to borrow ten dollars from her, I still tried to save face by telling her before long I would be in the money.

But continual lies grow stale, and after a while, I began to realize that when I told Nina a lie, she knew I was lying. She pretended to believe me, and that's where she went wrong. She should have called my bluff, and maybe I would have snapped out of this pipe dream of mine, but she didn't, so I went on drinking, went on lying and went on getting nowhere.

Then one afternoon while I was sitting in a bar facing the beach, this thing I want to tell you about started.

The time was a little before six o'clock. I was pretty sloshed. I had knocked back eight whiskies and was looking forward to the ninth.

The bar was small and quiet and not well patronized. I liked it. I could sit in a corner undisturbed and look out of the open window and watch the people enjoying themselves on the beach. I had been a regular customer now for five days. The barman, a big, fat, bald-headed guy, knew me. He seemed to understand my need for whisky. As soon as I finished one drink, he brought me another.

There weren't many drinkers in the bar. From time to time a man or a woman would come in, shoot a drink down their throats, hang around for a few minutes, then leave. They were like me — without an anchor, lonely and trying to kill time.

In a corner, near my table and out of sight of the bar was a telephone booth. There was a pretty regular traffic to the booth. People came in, made a call, then went out: men, women, boys and girls. The booth was the busiest place in the bar.

While I sat drinking, I watched the booth: it gave me something to do. I wondered a little drunkenly who these people were who shut themselves in behind the glass panelled door: who they were talking to. I watched their expressions. Some of them smiled as they talked: some got worked up: some of them looked as if they were telling unconvincing lies the way I had been telling unconvincing lies. It was like watching a stage play.

The barman brought me my ninth whisky and put it on the table. This time he stood by me, not moving, and I knew it was time to settle the check. I gave him my last five-dollar bill. He grinned sympathetically as he handed me the change.

11

The grin told me he knew a drunk when he saw one. I felt like getting up and driving my fist into his fat, stupid face, but I took the change and as I started to look for a small coin to tip him, his grin widened and he went back to the bar.

It was at this moment, when I realized he knew the kind of lush he was selling liquor to, that I felt pretty ashamed of myself. I felt so goddamed ashamed, I could have walked right out of the bar and under a fast moving car, but that kind of an end took guts, and I had left my guts in Cell 114. I wasn't walking in front of any fast moving car. I was just going to sit here and drink myself silly. It was better and easier that way.

Then a woman came into the bar. She walked to the telephone booth and shut herself in.

She was wearing a close-fitting canary coloured sweater and white slacks. She had on bottle green sun goggles, and she carried a yellow and white plastic handbag.

She immediately attracted my attention because she had solid, heavy hips and her slacks were tight fitting. As she walked to the telephone booth the movement of her *derriére* was something that even non-drinking and respectable men would have stared at.

I was a drinking, non-respectable man, so I stared without any inhibition. When I had lost sight of this portion of her body as she shut the telephone booth door, I lifted my eyes to look at her face.

She would be about thirty-three: a blonde with clear cut, somewhat cold features, but as a general ensemble she was very, very attractive to any male.

I drank half my ninth whisky and watched her use the telephone. I couldn't tell if her conversation was a happy one or not. The sun goggles made speculation impossible but she was quick and to-the-point. She was in the booth under a minute flat. She came out and walked past me, without looking at me. I stared at her straight back and the heavy curve of her hips for a brief, pleasant couple of seconds before she let the door swing behind her.

I was drunk enough to think that if I had been a single man, she would be the one I would have gone for. A woman, I reasoned to myself, with a figure like that, with her poise and looks must be sensational in bed. If she wasn't, then life was even a bigger illusion that.. I had imagined it to be.

I wondered who she was. Her clothes were expensive. The yellow and white handbag wasn't something you picked up in a junk shop.

The yellow and white handbag.

She had taken it into the telephone booth with her, but I couldn't remember her coming out with it.

I was now so sloshed, thinking became an effort. I screwed up my face, trying to remember. She had gone into the booth with the bag in her right hand. I was certain she had come out of the booth without anything in either hand.

I finished my whisky, then with a shaky hand, I lit a cigarette. So what? I said to myself. I had probably not noticed the bag when she came out.

Suddenly the bag became important to me. It became important because I wanted to prove to myself I wasn't as plastered as I thought I was.

I got unsteadily to my feet and walked to the telephone booth. I opened the door, and there on the shelf was the handbag.

Well, you old sonofabitch, I said to myself, you're as sober as a judge. You saw at once she had forgotten her bag. You're carrying your liquor like like... well, you're carrying your liquor.

The thing to do, I went on, talking to myself, is to look in the bag and find out who she is. Then you take the bag, telling the barman she has left it in the telephone booth you must tell him otherwise if you are spotted walking down the street with a lady's yellow and white handbag, some cop might pinch you — then when you have told the barman, you'll take the bag to her address and who knows — she might reward you with something more than a kiss who knows?

That's how drunk I was.

So I stepped into the booth and closed the door. I picked up the handbag and opened it. As I did so, I looked over my shoulder to make sure no one was watching me. Ex-jailbird Barber: that was me: taking no chances; always on the look out for trouble.

No one was watching me.

13

I turned my back which was broad enough to fill nearly all the booth, and picked up the telephone receiver; a smart move this — and resting the receiver against my ears, I examined the contents of the bag.

There was a gold cigarette case and a gold lighter. There was a diamond clip which could have been worth fifteen hundred dollars if not more. There was a driving licence. And there was a fat roll of bills and the top one was a fifty. If the others matched it, there could be close on two thousand dollars in that nice looking, juicy roll.

The sight of all that money brought me out in a sweat.

The cigarette case, the lighter and the diamond clip didn't interest me. All three could be traced, but I found myself being too interested in this fat roll of money.

With this money in my pocket, I wouldn't have to ask Nina for five bucks tomorrow morning. I wouldn't have to ask her for money neither tomorrow nor the day after, nor any time. I would be able to find a job by the time I had used up this money. Even if I kept on drinking, day in and night out.

I was plastered. I was not only plastered but I was demoralized. If this rich woman was so dumb as to leave the money right here, then she deserved to lose it.

Then far away, a faint voice that was my own said to me, 'Have you gone crazy? It's stealing! If they catch you with your record, you'll go away for ten years. Put the goddam bag down and get the hell out of here! What's the matter with you? Do you want ten more years in a cell?'

But the voice was too far away to make an impression. I wanted that money. It was easy. All I had to do was to take it out of the bag, put it in my pocket, close the bag, put it back on the shelf and fade away.

The barman couldn't see me. There was a continual stream of people going in and out of the booth. Anyone could have taken it — anyone.

The money was there — probably not two thousand dollars, but getting on that way.

I wanted it.

I needed it.

So I took it.

I dropped the roll into my pocket and shut the bag. My heart was thumping and I felt what I was — a thief. There was a tiny mirror above the telephone. I saw a movement in it. I still had the bag in my hand. I looked in the mirror.

She was right there behind me, watching me. Her sun goggles reflected the light so they made two little green spots in the mirror.

But she was there.

How long had she been there I didn't know.

But she was there.

CHAPTER TWO

I

WHEN you get a shock that squeezes your heart, paralyses your brain and turns your body cold, you die a little.

I stood looking into the mirror on the wall of the booth, the handbag gripped in my hand, staring at the two enormous green pieces of glass that formed her sun goggles, and I died a little.

I became suddenly sober. The whisky fumes that had clouded my brain went away: it was like a razor, slitting through gauze.

She would call the barman and he would find the roll of money in my pocket, then he would call a cop. Once the cop arrived, I would be a parcel of meat to be handled safely and surely back into a cell, but not for four years: it would be a much, much longer sentence this time.

Fingers tapped lightly on the glass door of the booth. I put the handbag on the shelf and turned, then I opened the door.

The woman moved slightly to one side to let me have room to come out.

'I think I left my handbag. . .' she said.

'That's right,' I said. 'I was going to give it to the barman.'

Maybe the best thing I could do was to push past her and get on to the street before she had time to open the bag and

15

find the money missing. Once I got on the street I could throw the money away, then it would be her word against, mine.

I started to make the move, then stopped. The barman had come from behind the counter and was blocking the exit. He was looking puzzled, and he came forward, still keeping his vast bulk between me and the door.

'Is this guy annoying you, lady?' he said to the woman.

She turned her head slowly. I had a feeling that whatever the emergency she would always remain poised and unruffled.

'Why, no. I stupidly left my handbag in the booth. This gentleman was going to give it to you to keep for me.'

The barman looked suspiciously at me.

'Is that a fact?' he said. 'Well, okay, if that's what he says.'

I just stood there like a dummy. My mouth was so dry I couldn't have spoken even if I had known what to say.

'Anything of value in the bag, lady?' the barman asked.

'Oh, yes. It was stupid of me to have forgotten it.' She had a clear, hard voice. I wondered vaguely if her eyes, hidden behind the sun goggles, were as hard.

'Hadn't you better check to see if anything is missing?' the barman said.

'I suppose I'd better.'

I wondered if one quick punch would get me out of this. I decided it wouldn't. The barman looked as if he had taken a lot of quick punches in his day, and he looked as if the diet had agreed with him.

She moved past me into the booth and picked up the bag.

I watched her, my heart scarcely beating. She stepped out of the booth, opened the bag and looked inside. With slim fingers, the nails painted silver, she moved the contents of the bag about, her face expressionless.

The barman breathed heavily. He kept glancing at me and then at her.

Here it comes, I thought. In half an hour from now, I'll be in a cell.

'No, there's nothing missing,' she said. She turned her head slowly to look directly at me. 'Thank you for taking care of it for me. I'm afraid I am very careless with my things.'

I didn't say anything.

16

The barman beamed.

'Okay, lady?'

'Yes, thank you. I think we might celebrate.' She looked at me. The round green globes of her goggles told me nothing. 'May I buy you a drink, Mr. Barber?'

So she knew who I was. It wasn't all that surprising. The day I had been released, the *Herald* had run a photograph of me, saying that I had been released from jail after spending a four-year stretch for a manslaughter charge. They hadn't forgotten to mention that I had been drunk at the time. It had been a good photograph and it had been on the front page where no one who read the *Herald* could miss it. Just a sweet trick that Cubitt would dream up.

There was a steely quality in her voice that told me it might be healthier for me to accept the invitation, so I said, 'Well, it isn't necessary, but thanks.'

She turned to the barman.

'Two highballs with lots of ice.'

She moved past him to the table where I had been sitting and sat down.

I sat opposite her.

She opened her handbag, took out the gold cigarette case, opened it and offered it to me.

I took a cigarette. She took one too. She lit mine with the gold lighter, then her own: by this time the barman had come back with two highballs. He put them on the table, then went away.

'How does it feel, Mr. Barber, to be out of prison?' she asked, letting smoke drift down her nostrils.

'All right.'

'I see you are no longer a newspaper man.'

'That's correct.'

She tilted the high glass, making the ice cubes tinkle and she regarded the glass as if it interested her more than I did.

'I've seen you come in here quite often.' She waved silver nails to the window. 'I have a beach cabin across the way.'

'That must be nice for you.'

She picked up her drink and sipped a little of the highball.

17

'Do these frequent visits to this bar mean you haven't fixed up a job. yet?'

"That's right.'

'Do you hope to get fixed up pretty soon?'

'That's right.'

'It can't be easy, of course.'

'That's right.'

'If employment was offered to you, would you be interested?'

I frowned at her.

'I don't get this. Are you offering me employment?'

'It is possible. Would you be interested?'

I reached for the highball, then changed my mind. I had had more than enough to drink.

'Doing what?'

'It would be very well paid, very confidential and with a small element of risk. Would that worry you?' 'You mean it would be illegal?'

'Oh no ... it wouldn't be illegal nothing like that.'

'That doesn't tell me anything. Where does the risk come in? I'm ready to do any job so long as I know what I am doing.'

'I understand.' She took another sip from the highball. 'You're not drinking, Mr. Barber.'

'I know. What's this job you want done?'

'I'm a little pressed for time right now, besides this is scarcely the place to discuss a confidential proposition, is it? Could I telephone you some time? We could meet somewhere more convenient.'

'I'm in the book.'

'Then I'll do that. Tomorrow perhaps. Will you be in?'

'I'll make a point of it.'

'I'll settle the check.' She opened her purse, then she paused, frowning. 'Oh, I was forgetting.'

'I wasn't.'

I took the roll of money from my pocket and dropped it into her lap.

'Thank you.' She flicked the fifty off, drew a five from under it and put the five on the table, then she dropped the roll into her bag, closed it and stood up.

18

I stood up too.

'Then tomorrow, Mr. Barber.'

She turned and walked out of the bar. I watched the heavy, sensual roll of her hips as she crossed the street. I went to the door and watched her walk leisurely to the car park. She got in a silver and grey Rolls-Royce and she drove away, leaving me staring after her, but not so startled as to forget to memorize her car number.

I went back to the table and sat down. My knees felt weak. I drank a little or the highball, then I lit a cigarette.

The barman came over and collected the five-dollar bill.

'Some dish,' he said. 'Looks loaded with dough. How did you make out with her? Did she give you a reward?' I stared at him for a long moment, then I got up and walked out. Just for the record, that was the last time I ever went in there. Even when I had to pass it, the sight of the place gave me a cold, sick feeling.

Across the way was the branch office of the A.A.A. The clerk in charge was a guy I had known well while I had worked for the *Herald*. His name was Ed Marshall. I crossed the road and went into the office.

Marshall was sitting at a desk, reading a magazine.

'Why, for the love of Mike!' he exclaimed, starting to his feet. 'How are you, Harry?'

I said I was fine and shook hands with him. I was pleased to get such a welcome: most of my so-called friends had given me the brush off when I had looked them up, but Marshall was a decent little guy: we had always got along together.

I sat on the edge of his desk and offered him a cigarette.

'I've given them up,' he said, shaking his head. 'This lung cancer has me scared. How's it feel to be out?'

'It's okay,' I said. 'You can get used to anything, even living out of jail.'

We talked of this and that for ten minutes or so, then I got around to the real reason why I had called on him.

'Tell me, Ed, who owns a grey and black Rolls. The number is SAXI?'

'You mean Mr. Malroux's car.'

'Do I? Is that his number'

19

'That's right: a honey of a car.'

Then the nickle dropped like a chunk of lead.

'You don't mean *Felix* Malroux?' I said, staring at him.

'That's him.'

'You mean he lives in Palm Bay? I thought he lived in Paris.'

'He bought a place here about two years ago. He came here for his health.'

I was now aware that my heart was thumping, and I had trouble in keeping and looking calm.

'We are talking about the same man? Malroux: the zinc and copper millionaire He must be one of the richest men in the world.'

Marshall nodded.

'He is. He's a pretty sick man from what I hear. I wouldn't swop places with him for all his dough.' 'What's the matter with him?'

Marshall grimaced.

'He's a lung cancer case. There's nothing anyone can do for him.'

I looked at my cigarette, then stubbed it out.

That's tough. So he's bought a place here?'

'Yep. He's bought East Shore: Ira Cranleigh's place. He's had it practically rebuilt. It's a wonderful situation: own harbour, own beach, own bathing' pool, own everything.'

I well remembered Ira Cranleigh's house. He had been a big oil operator and had built the house at the far end of the bay. He had got into a financial mess and had had to sell. The sale was being negotiated at the time of my trial.

I never had heard who had bought it.

I lit another cigarette while my brain jumped over hurdles and darted through hoops.

'So the Rolls is his?'

'Just one of about ten cars he owns.'

'It's a beaut. I'd like to own it myself.'

Marshall nodded his balding head.

'Me too.'

'Who would be the woman driving it? I couldn't see much of her. She was a blonde, wearing big sun goggles.'

'That'd be Mrs. Malroux.'

'His wife? She didn't look old I'd say she was around thirty-two or three. Malroux must be getting on. I seem to have been hearing about him ever since I was a kid. He must be pushing seventy or more.'

'About that. He married again: some woman he fell for in Paris. I forget who she was: a movie star or something. There was quite a write up about her in the *Herald.*'

'What happened to his first wife?'

'She had a car accident about three years ago.'

'So Malroux's here for his health?'

'That's it. His wife and daughter like living in California anyway, and the climate is supposed to be good for his health. That's the way the quacks talk: from what I hear, nothing now will be any good for him.'

'So he has a daughter?'

Marshall flicked his thumb, then stuck it in the air. 'He certainly has. From the first marriage: she's only a kid: eighteen, but some chicken.' He winked at me. 'I'd rather have her than the Rolls.'

'Hey! Yey! I thought you were a respectably married man.'

'So I am, but you want to see Odette Malroux. She'd make a corpse have wicked thoughts.'

'So long as you keep it to thoughts,' I said and slid off the desk 'I'd better get moving. I'm late as it is.'

'What's the interest in Malroux, Harry?'

'You know me: I saw the car and the woman. I was just curious.'

I could see I hadn't convinced him, but he didn't press it.

'If you happen to want a temporary job, Harry,' he said awkwardly, 'we're hiring guys to take a traffic count, starting from tomorrow. It pays fifty a week and lasts ten days. Any good to you?'

I didn't hesitate one second.

'That's nice of you, Ed, but I've got something lined up.' I grinned at him. 'Thank's all the same.'

In the bus, on the way home, I turned over in my mind the information I had got from Marshall. It excited me.

The wife of one of the richest men in the world had a job

for me. I had no doubt about it. She would telephone tomorrow. An element of risk, she had said. Well, okay, I was willing to take risks if the money was big enough, and it would be.

As the bus carried me along the beach road, I whistled under my breath.

This was the first time since I had gone to jail that I had felt like whistling.

Life was coming alive again.

II

Soon after nine o'clock the following morning, I went down to the offices of the *Herald*.

Nina had told me that she had some pots to deliver and she wouldn't be back until midday. This suited me. If Malroux's wife did telephone, I would have the place to myself. I certainly wasn't telling Nina what had happened until I knew what the job was going to be.

I walked into the reference room of the *Herald's* offices. There were two girls in charge. I had never seen them before, and they didn't know me. I asked one of them to let me have the back files of the *Herald* from January, two years back.

It didn't take me long to dig out the information I was looking for. I learned that Felix Malroux had married Rhea Passary five months after the death of his first wife. Rhea Passary had been a show girl at the Lido, Paris. After a whirlwind courtship that lasted scarcely a week, Malroux proposed and she accepted him. It was pretty obvious she wasn't accepting him but his money.

I returned home and sat down to wait. Exactly at eleven o'clock the telephone bell rang. I knew it was her before I lifted the receiver. My heart was beating fast and my hand as I reached for the receiver, was shaking.

'Mr. Barber?'

There was no mistaking that clear, hard voice.

"Yes,' I said.

'We met yesterday.'

I decided this was the time to slip in a fast one.

'Why, sure, Mrs. Malroux, at Joe's bar.'

22

It was a good one. There was a pause. I wasn't sure but I thought I heard her catch her breath sharply, but it could have been imagination.

'Do you know East Beach where the bathing cabins are?' she asked.

'Yes.'

'I want you to hire a cabin: the last cabin on the left. I will meet you there at nine o'clock tonight.'

'I'll hire the cabin, and I'll be there,' I said.

There was a pause while I listened to her breathing, then she said, 'Tonight then at nine,' and she cut the connection.

I replaced the receiver and lit a cigarette. I was excited. The situation intrigued me. *An element of risk.* It would be interesting to learn what she wanted. Maybe she was in some kind of jam — blackmail. Maybe she wanted me to help her get rid of an unwanted lover. I shrugged. It was no use speculating.

I looked at my wrist watch. The time was ten minutes past eleven. I would have time to take a bus out to East Beach, book the cabin and get back before Nina returned.

I went out there. The man in charge of the cabins was Bill Holden: a large muscular hunk of meat who was a life-saver as well as the cabin attendant.

The cabins at East Beach were the luxury kind. You could sleep there if you wanted to. They stood in a long row, facing the sea, and I could see at this hour most of them were occupied.

Holden knew me, and when he saw me, he grinned.

'Hello, Mr. Barber, glad to see you again.'

'Thanks.' I shook hands with him. 'I want to hire a cabin. The last one on the left. I'll need it tonight at nine. Can you fix it?'

'We shut at eight, Mr. Barber,' he said. 'There won't be anyone here, but you can have it. I've got no all-night customers this week so I'm not staying on. Okay?'

'That's all right. Leave the key under the mat. I'll settle up tomorrow.'

'Anything you say, Mr. Barber.'

I looked along the crowded beach. The sand was covered with near naked bodies.

23

'Looks as if you're doing all right" I said.

'I survive, although the season's not what it should be. The all-night let is a flop. If it doesn't pick up soon, I'm going to drop the idea. No point hanging around here after eight if I've got no customers. Arc you doing all right, Mr. Barber?'

'I'm not grumbling. Well, I'll be along tonight. See you in the morning.'

On my way back home, I puzzled my brains to know what to tell Nina. I had to give her a reason why I would be out this night. Finally, I decided to tell her I was working for Ed Marshall, doing night work, counting cars in the A.A.A. traffic check up.

When I did tell her, I felt a bit of a heel to see how pleased she was.

'I might as well pick up fifty a week,' I said, 'as sit around here doing nothing.' At half past eight that evening, I left the bungalow and went around to the garage. We owned an ancient Packard that was pretty well on its last legs. As I coaxed the engine to start, I told myself if this job paid off, the first thing I'd do would be to buy a new car.

I reached East Beach at three minutes to nine o'clock.

It was deserted. I found the key of the cabin under the mat and I unlocked the door.

There was a lounging room, a bedroom, a shower room and a kitchenette. The cabin was air-conditioned. It had a TV and radio set, a telephone and a bar. There was even a bottle of whisky and charge water on one of the shelves behind the bar, It was all very lush and plush.

I turned the air-conditioner off and opened the windows and the door. I sat on the veranda in one of the cane lounging chairs.

It was lonely and quiet. The only sound came from the gentle movement of the sea. I was pretty tense, wondering what this woman wanted me to do, wondering too how much she was willing to pay for what she wanted done.

I waited for twenty-five minutes. Then just as I was beginning to think she wasn't coming, she materialized out of the darkness. I didn't see her arrive. I was sitting there, just about to light a third cigarette, when I saw a movement. I looked up, and there she was: standing quite close to me.

'Good evening, Mr. Barber,' she said, and before I could move, she sat down in a lounging chair close to mine.

I could see little of her. She had a silk scarf over her head that partially concealed her face. She was wearing a dark red summer dress. Around her right wrist was a heavy gold bracelet.

'I know quite a lot about you,' she said. 'A man who will turn down a ten thousand dollar bribe and refuse to work with gangsters must have a nerve. I'm looking for a man with nerve.'

I didn't say anything.

She lit a cigarette. I was aware she was staring at me. She was sitting in the shadows. I would have liked to have been able to see the expression in her eyes.

'You take risks, don't you, Mr. Barber?'

'Do I?'

'When you took my money, you risked going to jail for at least six years.'

'I was drunk.'

'Are you willing to take a risk?'

'It depends on the money,' I said. 'I want money. I don't make any bones about it. I want it, I need it, and I'm willing to earn it, but it has to be money, not chick feed.'

'If you'll do what I want you to do, I will pay you fifty thousand dollars.'

It was like taking a hard punch under the heart.

'Fifty thousand.' Did you say *fifty thousand dollars?*'

'Yes. It's a lot of money, isn't it? I'll pay you that if you will do what I want you to do.'

I drew in a long slow breath.

Fifty thousand dollars! My heart began to thump at the thought of so much money.

'And what's that?'

'You sound interested, Mr. Barber. Would you take risks for such a sum?'

'I'd take a lot of risk.'

I was thinking what I could do with all that money.

Nina and I could leave Palm City. We could start a new life together.

'Before we go any further, Mr. Barber,' she said 'it's only fair to tell you I haven't any money except the allowance my husband makes me. My husband believes that his daughter and I should be able to manage on the allowance he provides. I admit they are generous allowances for reasonable people, but it so happens neither my stepdaughter nor I are reasonable people.'

'If you haven't the money, why offer me fifty thousand dollars?' I said impatiently.

'I can show you how you can make it.'

I stared at her and she stared at me.

'Tell me — how do I make it?'

'My stepdaughter and I need four hundred and fifty thousand dollars. We must have this money within two weeks. I am hoping you will help us get it, and if you do, you will be paid fifty thousand dollars.'

I studied her and decided she wasn't crazy. On the contrary, I had never seen a woman who looked more sane.

'But how do I do it?' I asked.

But she wasn't to be hurried.

'Of course my husband could provide the money without any difficulty,' she said. 'Naturally, he would want to know why we wanted such a sum, and that is something neither of us can tell him.' She paused to tap ash off her cigarette. "But with your help, we could get the money from my husband without having to answer awkward questions.'

My first surge of excitement was waning. This sounded like a confidence trick. I was now very alert.

'Why do you want all this money?' I asked.

'You were clever to find out who I am.'

'An idiot child could have found that out. If you want to remain anonymous, don't drive that Rolls. Are you being blackmailed?'

'That doesn't concern you. I have an idea to get this money, but I need your help, and I'm willing to pay you fifty thousand dollars.'

'Which you don't have.'

"But with your help, I shall have.'

I was liking this less and less.

'Let's get to the point. What is this idea of yours?'

'My stepdaughter is going to be kidnapped,' she told me

26

coolly. 'The ransom money will be five hundred thousand dollars. You will get ten per cent of that. My step daughter and I divide what is left.'

'Who will do the kidnapping?'

'Why, no one. Odette will go away somewhere, and you will make the ransom demand. That is why I need your help. You will be the threatening voice on the telephone. It is simple enough, but it will have to be well done. For making the telephone call, and for collecting the ransom, I am offering you fifty thousand dollars.'

Well, the cat was out of the bag now. I felt my mouth turn dry.

Kidnapping was a capital offence. If I was going to touch this job, I would have to be more than careful. A kidnapper went to the gas chamber if he was caught.

This idea of hers could be dangerous as murder — it carried the death sentence.

CHAPTER THREE

I

A SMALL dark cloud drifted across the face of the moon. For the space of a minute or so, the sea looked suddenly cold and the beach dark and uninviting, then the cloud passed and once more there was silver on the water and brightness on the beach.

Rhea Malroux was looking at me.

'There is no other way of raising such a sum,' she said. 'It will have to be kidnapping. It's the only way to make my husband part with the money. It is easy enough. It's just a matter of working out the details.'

'Kidnapping carries the death sentence,' I said. 'Have you thought of that?'

'But no one is being kidnapped,' she returned, and stretched out her long, beautiful legs. 'Just supposing something went wrong, then I will tell my husband the truth, and that will be that.'

27

To me, she was as convincing as a carpet salesman trying to sell me a fake Persian rug.

But at the back of my mind was tne thought of fifty thousand dollars. Maybe, I told myself, if I handled the set-up, worked out all the details myself, I could sink a hook into that money.

'You mean your husband will just laugh and tell you you and your stepdaughter are naughty girls and do nothing more about it? The fact that I have telephoned him, telling him his daughter has been kidnapped and demanding money, won't mean a thing — he'll treat it as a joke? You think he'll tell the Federal Agents this is just some fun dreamed up by his wife to rook him out of five hundred thousand dollars?'

There was a long pause, then she said, 'I don't like your tone, Mr. Barber. You are being impertinent.'

'So sorry, but I once was a newspaper man,' I said. 'I know, perhaps a lot better than you do, that if the daughter of Felix Malroux is kidnapped it will make headline news all over the world. It could turn out to be another Lindberg case.'

She shifted in her chair and I saw her hands turn into fists.

'You're exaggerating. I won't allow my husband to call in the police.' Her voice was sharp and impatient. 'The situation will be this: Odette will disappear. You will telephone my husband and tell him she has been kidnapped. She will be returned if my husband will pay five hundred thousand dollars. My husband will pay the money. You will collect it and Odette returns. That's all there is to it.'

'You mean that's all you hope there is to it,' I said.

She made an impatient movement.

'I know that's all there is to it, Mr. Barber. You tell me you are prepared to take a risk if you are well paid. I am offering you fifty thousand dollars. If that isn't enough, say so and I'll find someone else.'

'Will you?' I said. 'Don't kid yourself. You would have quite a time to find anyone to take on a job like this. I don't like any of it. There are all kinds of snags. Suppose your husband calls in the police, in spite of what yon say? Once you have the police in your hair you have them there until someone gets arrested and that someone could be me.'

'The police won't come into it. I've told you: I can handle my husband.'

I thought of an ageing millionaire, dying slowly of cancer. Maybe he had lost his grip on life. Maybe she was right. Maybe she had the power to persuade him to part with five hundred thousand dollars without a fight.

Maybe.. .'

But against this sudden prick of conscience was the thought that if this worked, I would own fifty thousand dollars.

Your stepdaughter agrees to this idea?'

'Of course. She needs the money as much as I do.'

I flicked my cigarette butt into the darkness.

'I'm warning you,' I said, 'if the Federal Agents get on to it, we'll all be in trouble.'

'I'm coming to the conclusion you're not the man I am looking for,' she said. 'I think we are wasting each other's time.'

I should have agreed with her and let her walk away into the darkness as silently as she had come, but there was this nagging thought in my mind of the fifty thousand dollars she was offering me. The amount fascinated me. I realized, as I sat there in the moonlight, that if the Police Commissioner had put on his desk fifty thousand dollars in new crisp bills I would have fallen for his bribe. I realized, with a sense of shock, that my integrity was proof against a bribe of ten thousand dollars, but not against an offer of fifty thousand dollars.

'I'm just warning you,' I said. 'You and your stepdaughter and I would feel pretty sick if we landed behind bars.'

'How many more times do I have to tell you? There is no question of that.' Her voice was stifled with irritated impatience. 'Can I rely on you or can't I?'

'You've given me the bare outlines of your idea. Suppose you tell me exactly what you want me to do,' I said, 'then I'll be able to decide.'

'Odette will disappear; you will telephone my husband.' Her voice was exasperated. 'You will tell him she has been kidnapped, and she will be returned on payment of five hundred thousand dollars. You will make my husband believe that if he doesn't pay the ransom Odette won't be returned. You will have to be convincing, but I am relying on you for that.'

29

'Does your husband scare easily?' I asked. 'He is very fond of his daughter,' she said quietly. 'In these circumstances, he will scare easily.'

'Then what do I do?'

'You arrange how he is to pay the money. You collect it, you take your share and give the rest to me.' 'And your stepdaughter, of course.'

She paused before she said, 'Yes, of course.'

'It sounds pretty simple,' I said. 'The one snag is you may not know your husband as well as you imagine you do. He may not scare easily. He may call in the police. A man who has made the fortune he has must have plenty of what it takes. Have you considered that?'

'I told you: I can handle him.' She drew on her cigarette so the glowing tip lit up her glistening red mouth. 'He is ill. Two or three years ago, this wouldn't have been possible. A very sick man, Mr. Barber, hasn't much resistance when someone he loves seems to be in danger.'

I had a slightly sick feeling to imagine that but for the grace of God this woman could have been my wife.

'You probably know more about that than I do,' I said.

Again there was a pause. I could feel her hostility as she stared towards me out of the darkness.

'Well? Are you going to do it or aren't you?'

Again I thought of the fifty thousand dollars. This wasn't something to rush into, but given thought, given a detailed plan, it might possibly work.'

'I want to think about it. I'll give you a definite decision tomorrow.'

She got to her feet. Opening her bag, she took out a small roll of bills and dropped them on the table that stood between us.

'This should cover the cost of the cabin and any other expenses you may have. I'll telephone tomorrow.'

She went away as silently as she had come disappearing into the darkness like a ghost.

I picked up the money she had left on the table. There were ten ten-dollar bills. I slid them through my fingers, multiplying them in my mind five hundred times.

The time was now ten minutes after ten. I had a couple of hours yet before I need return home. I sat there in the moonlight, staring at the sea and I considered her proposal. I considered it from every angle – particularly the risk involved.

A few minutes after midnight, I made my decision. It wasn't an easy one to make, but I was influenced by the money she was offering me. With that sum I could make a new life for Nina and myself.

On my terms, and my terms only, I decided to do what she wanted me to do.

The following morning, I went down to the cabin early. I told Bill Holden I wanted to keep the cabin on for at least another day, possibly longer, and I paid him the rent for two days.

I sat in the sun outside the cabin until a few minutes to eleven then I went in and sat by the telephone. Exactly at eleven o'clock the telephone bell rang. I picked up the receiver.

'Barber here,' I said.

'Is it yes or no?'

'Yes yes,' I said 'but there are conditions. I want to talk to you and the other party. Come here with her at nine o'clock tonight.'

I didn't give her a chance to argue. I hung up. I wanted her to realize that the initiative had passed from her to me now, and it was going to stay that way.

The telephone bell rang, but I didn't answer. I went out of the cabin, shut and locked the door.

The bell was still ringing as I walked away to where I had parked the Packard.

II

I returned to the cabin just after six. I had been home and had collected a number of articles. Nina had been out which was lucky for me as she would have wanted to know why I needed a long length of flex, my tool kit and the tape recorder I had bought When I was working for the *Herald* and which she had kept for me all this time.

The two hours I had spent the previous night examining

Rhea Malroux's plan hadn't been wasted. I had quickly realized that it was essential for my safety to make absolutely certain neither Rhea nor her stepdaughter left me holding the baby if anything happened to go wrong. I had decided to make a record of our conversation this night: neither of them would know of the recording, but if Malroux did call in the police, and there was always that risk, then these two couldn't deny knowing anything about the plan nor shunt the blame on to me.

When I reached the cabin, I took the recorder into the bedroom and put it in the closet. The machine ran pretty silently, but there was just a chance one of them on the alert might hear it if it was in the sitting-room. I bored a small hole in the back of the closet through which I passed the mains lead. This I took into the sitting-room and plugged into a two-way adaptor that was controlled by the switch at the door. I satisfied myself that when I entered the cabin and turned on the light, the recorder and light in the sitting-room would be switched on simultaneously.

I spent some minutes trying to make up my mind where to conceal the microphone. I finally decided to fix it under a small occasional table that stood in a corner, out of the way, but with an uninterrupted field of sound.

All this took time. By seven o'clock, I had had a practice run and I was satisfied the recorder worked as I wanted it to work, and the microphone picked up the sound of my voice from any part of the room.

The only two snags I could think of were if the two women wouldn't go into the cabin, and if they didn't want the light on. I thought I would be able to persuade them to enter the cabin. I could point out someone might be out for an evening stroll and might spot us if we didn't keep out of sight. If they wanted the light out, I could turn the lamp off by the switch on the lamp and not by the switch at the door.

There were still a number of people on the beach, but the crowd was thinning. In another hour, the beach would be deserted.

I was just gathering up my tools when there came a knock on the door. I had been so preoccupied with what I had been doing the sharp rap made me start. For a moment I stood staring at the door. Then I shoved my tool kit under a cushion and went to the door. I opened it.

Bill Holden stood there.

'Sorry to disturb you, Mr. Barber,' he said. 'I wanted to know if you're keeping the cabin on for tomorrow. I have had an inquiry for it.'

'I want to keep it for a week, Bill,' I said. 'I'm writing a few articles and it is a good place for me to work. I'll settle with you at the end of the week, if that's okay with you.' 'Sure thing, Mr. Barber. It's yours until the end of the week.'

When he had gone, I collected my tool kit, locked up and went over to the Packard. I didn't feel like going home so I drove to a sea food restaurant about half a mile down the road. By the time I had eaten, the hands of my watched showed twenty minutes to nine.

It was getting dark.

I drove back to the cabin. The beach was now deserted. I remembered not to turn on the light. I could just see my way to the air-conditioner which I put on. I wanted the cabin to be invitingly cool when they arrived. Out on the veranda it was hot: too hot for comfort, but I loosened my tie and sat out there in a lounging chair.

I was pretty tense, and I wondered if Rhea would be late again, and what the stepdaughter Odette, would be like.

I wondered too, after they had listened to what I was going to say, if they would have the nerve to go ahead with this plan.

A few minutes after nine, I heard a sound and looking quickly to my left, I saw Rhea Malroux coming up the three steps to the veranda. She was alone.

I got to my feet.

'Good evening, Mr. Barber,' she said, moving towards one of the chairs.

'Let's go inside,' I said. 'Someone passed just now. We shouldn't be seen together.' I opened the cabin door and turned on the light, 'Where's your stepdaughter?'

She followed me into the cabin and I closed the door.

'She'll be along, I suppose,' she said indifferently. She sat down in one of the lounging chairs. She was wearing a pale

33

blue, sleeveless dress. Her slim legs were bare and she had on flat-heeled sandals. She took off the scarf that covered her head and shook free her sable-dyed hair with a quick jerk of her head. She still wore the green sun goggles and these she kept on.

'I'm not touching this job until I've talked to her,' I said. 'I want to be sure, Mrs. Malroux, that she knows about this kidnapping idea and she agrees to it.'

Rhea looked sharply at me.

'Of course she agrees to it,' she said curtly. 'What do you mean?'

'I want to hear her say it herself,' I said and sat down. Then speaking entirely for the benefit of the tape recorder, I went on, 'It's not an unreasonable request. You tell me you and your stepdaughter have concocted a plan where your stepdaughter pretends to be kidnapped. You two are urgently in need of four hundred and fifty thousand dollars. The only way you can get this sum from your husband is to fake a kidnapping. If I help you, you will pay me fifty thousand dollars.' I paused, then went on, 'Kidnapping is a capital offence. I want to be absolutely sure your stepdaughter knows what she is doing.'

Rhea said impatiently, 'Of course she knows what she is doing ... she isn't a child.'

"And you are satisfied your husband won't call in the Police?' I said.

She began to drum on the arm of her chair.

'You seem to have a natural talent for wasting time,' she said. 'We've been all over this before, haven't we?'

I was satisfied. With that short conversation on tape, she now couldn't deny being implicated if we hit trouble.

I looked at my watch: the time was half past nine.

'I'm not discussing this job nor am I touching it until I can talk to your stepdaughter,' I said.

Rhea lit a cigarette.

'I told her to come,' she said, 'but she seldom does what she is told. You don't expect me to drag her here, do you?'

I heard the sound of someone moving about outside.

'Maybe this is her now,' I said. 'I'll see.'

I went to the door and opened it.

A girl stood on the bottom of the steps, looking up at me. For a long moment, we stared at each other.

'Hello,' she said and she smiled at me.

Odette Malroux was small and finely made. She was wearing a feather-weight cashmere white sweater and a pair of leopard skin patterned jeans. Her outfit was calculated to show off the shape of her body. She had raven black hair, like Nina's, which was parted in the centre and fell to her shoulders in a careless but effective way. Her face was heart shaped and her complexion pallid. She could be any age from sixteen to twenty-five. Her eyes were slate grey. Her nose was pinched and small. Her mouth was a careless crimson gash of lipstick. She gave out an over-all picture of corrupt youth. You can find girls exactly like her in any juvenile court: defiant, rebellious, frustrated, sexually blasé, heading nowhere: one of the legion of the young lost.

'Miss Malroux?'

She giggled, then came up the steps, slowly.

'You must be Ali Baba — how are all the thieves?'

'Oh, come on in, Odette,' Rhea called impatiently. 'Save your wit for your moronic friends.'

The girl wrinkled her nose, making a grimace, then she winked at me. She moved past me into the cabin. She had a deliberately cultivated duck-tail walk. Her neat little behind moved as if on a swivel.

I closed the door.

I was thinking of the recorder. The tape had about forty minutes to run. I would have to hurry-this up if I was to get the whole conversation recorded.

'Hello, darling Rhea,' Odette said, dropping into a lounging chair near the chair where I had been sitting. 'Isn't he gorgeous?'

'Oh, shut up!' Rhea snapped. 'Be quiet and listen. Mr. Barber wants to talk to you.'

The girl looked at me and fluttered her eyelids. She drew up her legs under her, put one hand on her hip and the other to support her face and became mockingly grave.

'Please do talk to me. Mr. Baba.'

I looked into the slate grey eyes. The juvenile pose didn't

35

kid me for a moment. Those eyes were a complete give away — something she couldn't conceal. They were the unhappy, puzzled eyes of a girl who wasn't sure of herself, knew she was going the, wrong way, and not strong enough to do anything about it.

'I want to hear this direct from you,' I said. 'Are you a party to this kidnapping idea?'

The girl looked swiftly at Rhea and then at me.

'A party to it?' She giggled. 'Isn't he a doll, darling Rhea? Yes, of course, I'm a party to it. Darling Rhea and me thought it up between us. It's a great idea, isn't it?'

'Is it?' I stared at her. 'Your father mightn't think so.'

'That's no concern of yours,' Rhea snapped. 'Now, if you are satisfied, perhaps we can discuss this thing.'

'We can talk about it,' I said. 'When does it happen?'

'As soon as it can be arranged — the day after tomorrow perhaps,' Rhea said.

'Miss Malroux disappears — where is she disappearing to?'

'Call me Odette,' the girl said, and she pushed her chest out at me. 'All my friends do. . .'

Ignoring her, Rhea said, 'There is a quiet small hotel at Carmel. She can go there. It will only be for three or four days.

'How will she get there?' Rhea moved impatiently. 'She has a car.'

'It's a honey,' Odette told me. 'AT.R.3. It goes like the wind...'

'You can't drive a car like that without being recognized,' I said. 'You must be a familiar figure to people living here.'

She looked a little startled as she said, 'I suppose I am.'

I looked across at Rhea.

'Your idea, of course, is that only you, your stepdaughter and your husband are to know about this kidnapping?'

She frowned at me.

'Of course.'

'Is it all that simple for you to disappear?' I said to Odette. 'Haven't you any friends? How about the servants?'

She lifted her slim shoulders.

'I'm always going away.'

I looked at Rhea.

If I were in your husband's place and someone telephoned me that my daughter had been kidnapped and to get her back I had to pay out five hundred thousand dollars, I wouldn't be in too great a hurry to pay up. The way you plan it, there is no atmosphere. If I were your husband I might even think it was a hoax.' I stubbed out my cigarette, then went on, 'And I would call the police.'

'A lot depends on how convincing you are when you telephone him,' Rhea said. 'That's what I'm paying you for.'

'I'll be convincing,' I said, 'but suppose he does call in the police? What are you going to do? Tell him it's a joke? Admit you two were just having a bit of fun or will you say nothing and hope I'll get the money and the police won't find out the truth?'

'I keep telling you. . .'she began angrily.

'I know what, you tell me,' I said, but I don't have to believe you. If the police come into this, will you call it off or will you still go ahead?'

'We go ahead,' Odette said. 'We must have the money.

There was a sudden hard note in her voice that made me look sharply at her. Her face had a bleak expression and she wasn't looking at me, she was staring at Rhea.

'Yes,' Rhea said, 'we must have the money, but for the hundredth time, the police won't come into it!'

'It will be a lot safer to assume they will,' I said. 'Okay, it is possible your husband will hand over the ransom, but when he gets his daughter back, he is practically certain to tell the police and they will investigate. A man who has made as much money as your husband isn't a fool. How do you know he won't arrange to have the money marked? What use would it be to you if you didn't dare spend it?'

'I'll see he doesn't do that,' Rhea said. 'That is something we don't have to worry about.'

'Is it? I'd like to share your confidence.'

'My husband is very ill,' Rhea said, her voice hard and bleak, 'He does what I tell him to.'

I felt a chill crawl up my spine as I looked from her to Odette. Both of them were staring at me. The girl had lost her 'little-girl' pose. She seemed suddenly as hard and as ruthless as the older woman.

37

'I'm going to assume your husband will contact the police,' I said. 'If you don't like the way I've planned this thing, say so and I'll quit.'

Rhea's hands were fists in her lap. Odette was nibbling at her thumbnail: her eyes intent.

I spoke directly to her.

'Today is Tuesday. We can be ready by Saturday. I want you to arrange to go to a movie with a girl friend on Saturday evening. Can you fix that?'

I could see the surprise in her eyes as she nodded.

'I want you to have dinner at home and I want you to tell your father where you are going. I want you to wear something distinctive so you will be noticed and recognized when you go out. You will arrange to meet your friend at eight o'clock but you won't meet her. You will drive to the Pirates' Cabin. It's a small bar and restaurant about a couple of miles from here. Maybe you know it?' Again she nodded.

'You will drive into the parking lot and you'll go into the bar for a drink. At that time the place will be crowded. I don't imagine you're likely to run into any of your friends there' What do you think?'

'Not à chance,' she said. 'It's not the sort of place my friends would go to.'

'That's the: way I figured it. I want you to be noticed. Upset your drink or do something to attract attention in an accidental way. You will leave after five minutes. Be careful not to get involved with anyone. I'll have my car in the parking lot. Make sure no one is watching you, then get into my car. There will be a change of clothes in the car and a red wig. You'll put on the clothes and the wig.

'While you are changing, I will take your car and drive it to Lone Bay parking lot. You'll follow me. I'll leave your car in the parking lot. The chances are it won't be spotted until we need it again.

'You'll pick me up and I'll drive you to the airport. I'll have a reservation for you to Los Angeles. You will go to a hotel where there will be a reservation for you. You will tell the clerk you aren't well. You'll stay in your room, having all your meals sent up until I tell you to come back. I'll keep in touch with you by telephone. Do you follow all that?'

She nodded. She had stopped nibbling at her thumb.

She looked intrigued

'All this is entirely unnecessary,' Rhea said. 'If she goes to the hotel at Carmel...'

'Do you want this money or don't you?' I broke in.

'Must I repeat every statement I make to you?' she said angrily. 'I have said I want it!'

'Then you do it my way or you won't get it!'

'I think he's an absolute doll,' Odette said. 'I'll do whatever you say, Harry ... I may call you Harry?'

'You can call me what you like so long as you do what I tell you,' I said, then to Rhea, I went on, 'When I've seen Odette off on the plane, I will telephone your husband. He is a millionaire What chance have I got to get to him?'

'His secretary will answer,' Rhea said. 'If you tell him you want to talk to my husband about his daughter, his secretary will ask him if he wants to speak to you. I will be there. I'll see my husband does speak to you.'

'It will be late. I'm hoping Odette's girl friend will have telephoned asking where she has got to.' I looked at Odette. 'Do you think she will telephone?'

'Of course she will.'

'I want her to. It will create the right atmosphere. You must be missing before I telephone.'

'She'll call,' Odette said.

'Okay. I'll tell your father to have the money ready in two days' time and to wait for further instructions,' I said, then looked over at Rhea. 'You must persuade him not to try any tricks. What you have to be careful about is that he doesn't tell the bank to take the numbers of the bills or get the Federal Bureau to mark the money. How you do that, I wouldn't know, but if you don't fix it, you won't be able to spend the money — nor shall I.'

'I'll arrange it,' Rhea said curtly.

'I hope you will. Two days after my first telephone call, I'll call again. Is your husband well enough to deliver the ransom himself?'

She nodded.

'He wouldn't trust anyone to do it except himself.'

39

I lifted my eyebrows at her.

'Not even you?'

Odette giggled, putting her hand over her mouth, while Rhea's eyes narrowed and her face hardened.

'Of course he trusts me!' she said angrily, 'but he would consider it dangerous. He wouldn't allow me to go with him.'

'Well, okay.' I lit another cigarette. 'I'll tell him to leave home at two in the morning and drive along East Beach Road. He is to drive the Rolls. There'll be no traffic on that road at that time. The money is to be in a brief-case. Somewhere along the road he will see a flashing light. As he passes the light he is to drop the case out of the car and drive on. He is not to stop. In the meantime, Odette will have returned. She will come here to this cabin and wait for me. I will take my share of the money and give her the rest. What you two do with it after doesn't concern me, but you'll have to be careful.'

'Oh no!' Rhea said sharply. 'I'm not agreeing to that! You're not to give her the money! You're to give it to me!'

Odette sat up, swinging her legs to the floor. Her pallid face was puckered with spite.

'Why shouldn't he give it to me?' she demanded shrilly.

'Do you imagine I trust you?' Odette said, her voice hard and vicious. 'Once you get your claws into that money...'

'All right, all right cut it out!' I broke in. 'We're wasting time. Here's a better way. I'll draft a letter for Odette to write to her father. It'll be more convincing that way and will save me a third telephone call. She will tell him how to deliver the ransom. She will say, after he has delivered it, for him to drive on to Lone Bay parking lot where she will be waiting for him. It's a good half hour's drive. That'll give you both time to be here and collect the money. How's that?'

'But if Daddy finds I'm not at the parking lot, he might go to the police,' Odette said.

That was the first sensible thing either of them had volunteered since they had entered the cabin.

'That's right. Then in the letter he will be told there is a note waiting for him at Lone Bay, telling him where to find you. I'll put the note in your car. When he gets it, he'll be told you have returned home. That fix it?'

40

Rhea was staring at me.

'We shall, of course, have to trust you with all that money, Mr. Barber.'

I grinned at her.

'If that's going to worry you then you shouldn't have picked on me. If you have a better idea, now's the time to trot it out.'

The two women looked at each other, then Rhea, hesitating for a moment, said, 'So long as I am here when you hand over the money, I have no better suggestion.'

'That's another way of saying she trusts you and not me,' Odette said. 'Isn't she a lovely stepmother?'

'She has to trust me,' I said. 'Now you tell me something: what happened to you? Why didn't you meet your friend at the movies? Why did you go to the Pirates' Cabin? Who kidnapped you?'

She stared blankly at me.

'I wouldn't know. Why ask me? It's your story.'

'Don't you think you'd better know? Your father will question you. You can bet he will call in the police after he has got you back, and they will question you. Those boys are professionals. If they once suspect you're lying, they'll rip into you until they get the truth out of you.'

She lost a lot of her poise then and she looked uneasily at Rhea.

'But I'm not going to be questioned by the police! Rhea says I'm not!'

'Of course she isn't!' Rhea broke in.

'You both seem pretty certain of that,' I said. 'I'm not so sure.'

'My husband has a horror of publicity,' Rhea said. 'He would rather lose the money than get newspaper reporters worrying him.'

'Sorry, I'm still not convinced. I wouldn't be earning what you're going to pay me,' I said, 'if I didn't take the police into consideration. She must have a story ready in case the police move in. I'll fix it for her.' To Odette, I went on, 'Can you come out here tomorrow night so I can coach you? You'll need a lot of coaching if you want to keep that money.'

'It's not necessary,' Rhea said. 'How many more times do I have to tell you: my husband 'won't call in the police!'

41

'I told you I'd take this job on my own terms. You either do what I say or I'll quit,' I said.

'I'll be here tomorrow night at nine,' Odette said and smiled at me.

'That's that then.' I got to my feet. 'Just one more thing.' I was speaking to Rhea. 'You're to get her a dress. Get it from a cheap store: something a college girl would wear, and you've got to get her a red wig. Be careful how you get it. Don't get it at a local shop. Maybe it would be better if you went into Dayton for it. It mustn't be traced back to you. She's got to disappear completely at the Pirates' Cabin. She'll be seen there, and she'll be seen leaving, but after that there must be no trace of her until she returns home.'

Rhea shrugged.

'If you think this is really necessary, I'll do it.'

'Bring the dress and the wig with you tomorrow night,' I said to Odette. 'By then I'll have a story ready for you, and the letter.' I went to the door, opened it and looked out. The beach was deserted. 'See you tomorrow night.' Rhea went first, not looking at me. Odette followed her. As she passed me, she gave me a half smile and fluttered her eyelids at me.

I watched them walk away into the darkness, then I went into the bedroom and turned off the tape recorder.

CHAPTER FOUR

1

AT a few minutes after nine o'clock the next evening, Odette came out of the darkness and paused at the foot of the steps to look up at me.

There was a big moon and I could see her clearly.

She was wearing a simple, full skirted white frock , She carried a suitcase. She looked very attractive as she stood there, looking up at me.

'Hello, Harry,' she said. 'Well, here I am.'

I went down the steps and took the suitcase from her. I was a little disturbed that she was alone.

'We'll go inside,' I said. 'Isn't Mrs. Malroux coming?' The girl gave me a sidelong glance and she smiled.

'Was she invited? Anyway she isn't coming.'

Together, we went into the cabin. I shut the door, then turned on the light. I had a new tape on the recorder. As I turned on the light, the recorder in the bedroom began to record.

I had had a busy day, working out the details I wanted the girl to learn. I had the letter drafted for her. I had played back the tape and had satisfied myself that the recording couldn't have been better. I had made a parcel of it and had lodged it in my bank.

I was now pretty confident, and the itch to lay my hands on that fifty thousand dollars was really something.

I was certain I couldn't be prosecuted if anything went wrong unless both the girl and Rhea were prosecuted too, and I couldn't imagine Malroux prosecuting his wife and daughter, so that had to let me out if we ran into trouble.

'Let's go,' I said, sitting down. There's a lot to do and we haven't much time.'

I watched her walk over to the settee and sit down. Her movements were provocative, and I found myself watching her a little too intently. She drew up her legs under her, adjusted her skirts and then looked inquiringly at me. That look made me uneasy. This girl knew her way around. She knew too she was making an impression on me.

'I think Rhea was very clever to trap you into helping us,' she said. 'But you could be even more clever than she is.'

I stiffened.

'She didn't trap me into anything — what do you mean?'

'Oh, but she did. She had been' watching you for days, knocking back whisky in that bar. She had picked on you to help us as soon as she had read you had come out of jail. It was her idea to plant her handbag in the telephone booth. She was sure you would take her money. I said you wouldn't. We bet on it. I lost ten dollars.'

I sat there staring at her, feeling the blood burning my face.

'I was drunk,' I said.

43

She shrugged her shoulders.

'I'm sure you were. I'm just telling you this so you can be on your guard. Rhea is a snake: don't trust her further than you can throw her.'

'Just why do you want all this money?'

She wrinkled her nose at me.

'That's not your business. Now tell me, what am I to do? Have you got a story ready for me?'

I stared at her for a long moment, trying to collect my thoughts. This news that Rhea had planted her bag shook me. I told myself I would have to watch her.

I said, 'Have you fixed the date for Saturday?'

'Yes. My friend, Mauvis Sheen, and I are going to a movie at the Capital. I've arranged to meet her outside at nine.'

'Have you a boy friend you go around with from time to time? I don't mean a regular one. I mean someone you see only now and then?'

She looked puzzled.

'Well, yes. There are a number of them.'

'One will do — give me a name.'

'Well, there's Jerry Williams.'

'Does he ever telephone you at home?'

'Yes.'

'Who answers the telephone when anyone calls?'

'Sabin — he's the butler.'

'Would he know Williams's voice?'

'I don't think so. Jerry hasn't called me now for a couple of months.'

'What I'm getting at is this: you will tell your father you are going to the movies with your girl friend. After dinner, around eight-forty-five, I'll telephone and ask for you. I'll tell your butler it is Jerry Williams calling. I'm doing this entirely to take care of the police in case they come into it. Speaking as Williams, I will tell you that I have met your girl friend and we, with some other kids, are going to have a night out at the Pirates' Cabin. We want you to join us. You'll be surprised, but you'll agree, but you won't tell anyone where you are going because you will know your father will disapprove of you going to such a joint. You'll arrive there, you won't find your friends,

44

and you'll leave. As you are crossing the dark car park, a rug will be thrown over your head and you will be bundled into a car. Do you follow all this?'

She nodded.

"My goodness! You are taking this seriously, aren't you?'

'I'm taking it seriously because it happens to be serious,' I said. 'The police, if they come into it, will check with Williams, but he'll swear he didn't telephone you, and they'll realize it was a trick by the kidnappers to get you to the Pirates' Cabin. They'll wonder why you didn't recognize Williams's voice. You'll say the connection was bad, there was a lot of background noises of music and you never doubted it was Williams talking That's the explanation why you went to the Pirates' Cabin. Okay?'

'You don't really think the police will come into it?'

She was nibbling at her thumbnail while she stared at me.

'I don't know. Your stepmother said they won't, but I am going to be prepared. Now concentrate. I'm giving you the story you may have to tell the police. You are now in a car with the rug over you and you are held down by threatening hands. A man, speaking with an Italian accent, warns you if you make a sound, you'll get hurt. You gather that there are three men in the car. I've written down a conversation you overhear. You'll have to learn it by heart.

'The car makes a number of turns which leads you to believe you are off the main roads. Finally, after two hours driving, the car stops-. You hear a dog barking. You hear the sound of a gate being opened. The car drives forward and stops again. You must remember all these details. If the Federal Bureau come in on this, they'll want these details. Many a time they have caught kidnappers because the victim has heard a dog bark or has heard the noise a bucket makes going down into a well — stuff like that, and they'll probe your memory, so you've got to be ready for them.'

Her eyes were very intent as she nodded.

'I see now why you wanted me here tonight,' she said. 'Even if the police don't come into this, Daddy will ask questions. He is very shrewd. He will ask just those kind of questions.'

45

'Yes. You'll be supposed to be in this place for three days and nights. You'll be locked in a room. If the police come into this, they'll be certain to ask you to make a plan of the room and you must be able to do it without hesitation. During the time you're supposed to be in this room, you will hear the dog barking, you will hear the sound of chickens and cows. You'll decide this is a rundown farmhouse. You'll only see one of the kidnappers and a woman who will take charge of you. I've written down a description of both these people, and you've got to memorize it. If the police come into it, watch out you stick to your story. Don't let them trap you into mistakes.'

She was interested and very tense.

'I understand.'

'There is a toilet just outside the room you are in. This is just the kind of trap question they might spring on you, and you must be prepared for it. You're allowed to go there when you want. The woman takes you. I have another plan to show you the part of the house you will see when you go to the toilet. It's not much: a short passage and three doors that are shut. The toilet has a cracked basin and a string instead of a chain for the flush. Remember these details. They'll help to make your story convincing. I've written down all the meals you are supposed to eat during the three days you are in this farmhouse. You must memorize them too. Make no mistake about it, the Federal Agents will really turn you inside out if they come into this, and you've got to be ready for them.'

She touched her lips with the tip of her tongue.

'You're beginning to make me feel as if I'm really going to be kidnapped,' she said.

'That's the way you've got to feel I told her. 'I've drafted a letter you must write which I will mail to your father. You'd better do it now.'

I got up and went over to the briefcase I had brought with me. Before touching the sheets of cheap notepaper I had bought at a store, I put on a pair of gloves.

She came over to the table and sat down. I stood over her and watched her copy out the letter and finally address the envelope. I made her fold the letter and put it into the envelope and then put the envelope into my briefs case.

I then handed her the sheets of paper containing all the details I had prepared for her.

'Take this away and really memorize it,' I told her. 'Come here at nine o'clock the night after this, and I'll check you, then we're ready to go.'

She put the papers in her handbag.

'Before you go, let's look at the dress you have and. I want to see you in the wig.

She opened the case and took out a cheap blue and white print dress, white ballet shoes and a henna coloured wig.

I nodded to the bedroom door.

'Go in there and change. I want to see how you look.'

'For someone in my stepmother's employ,'- she said, picking up the dress, 'you certainly know how to give orders.'

'If you don't like it.'

'But I do! It makes a refreshing change.' She fluttered her eyelids at me. 'I like men older than myself.'

'That gives you a wide choice,' I said. 'Get moving. I want to get home.'

She wrinkled her nose at me, then went into the bedroom and shut the door.

I now became even more conscious that I was alone with this girl. She had that something that raised the worst in me: that would raise the worst in any man. Since I had been married, I had never fooled around with another woman and I wasn't intending to now although I knew this girl would be easy. I had only to give her some encouragement, and she would give me the green light to go the whole way.

There was a delay while I prowled around the room, then the bedroom door opened and she came out. The red wig made a startling difference to her appearance. I scarcely recognized her. She was holding the front of the dress up with her hands:

'The damn thing has a zipper.' She turned, showing me her naked back down to her waist. 'Zip me up, will you? I can't reach it.'

I took hold of the zipper. My hand was unsteady. My fingers touched the cool flesh of her back. She looked over her shoulder at me. There was that thing in her eyes. I pulled up the zipper. My heart was beginning to thump. She turned and moved against me, sliding her arms around my neck.

47

Just for a brief moment I surrendered to the pressure of her body against mine, then with a conscious effort, I shoved her away.

'That's something we don't do,' I said. 'Let's keep this strictly business.'

She put her head on one side as she stared at me.

'Don't you like me then?'

'I think you're cute. Let's leave it at that.' She made a little grimace, then moved under the light.

'Well? Do I pass?'

'Yes. If you wear pair of sun goggles, no one would know you.' I took out my handkerchief and wiped my sweating hands. 'Okay, get changed. Leave the dress and wig here. We'll meet again the night after next at nine.' She nodded and went into the bedroom, leaving the door ajar.

I lit a cigarette and sat on the edge of the table. I was still pretty worked up.

Then she called, 'Harry... I can't get this zipper undone.'

I hesitated for a brief moment, then I mashed out my cigarette. I didn't move, but I was aware my heart was pounding.

'Harry...'

I stood up, silently crossed to the cabin door and turned the key. Then I turned off the light and went into the bedroom.

II

John Renick's Buick stood outside my bungalow as, I swung the Packard through the open gates and into my garage.

The sight of the Buick gave me a hell of a jolt. I hadn't seen nor heard from Renick since he had picked me up outside the jail gates, weeks ago, and I had forgotten about him.

What was he doing here?

My mind was suddenly flustered. Nina would have told him that I had this traffic censor job. If it crossed his mind, he could easily find out I was lying about the job. Contact with anyone connected with the police was the last thing I wanted, now I was about to swing this fake kidnapping.

Besides, I was suffering from a guilty conscience. I was

regretting this lapse of mine with Odette. I was now sure she had given herself to me to show me her power and her contempt of men. Our love-making — if you can call it that — had been nothing but an explosion of physical violence. She had slid away from me, and dressed hurried in the dark, humming a jazz tune under her breath, ignoring me.

'I'll see you the night after tomorrow,' she had said out of the darkness. 'Bye for now,' and she had gone, leaving me still on the bed, ashamed and angry with myself, and hating her.

When I heard the cabin door slam shut after her, I got off the bed and turned off the recorder. I had taken the tape and put it in its container. Then I had taken a shower and then had gone into the sitting-room and had drunk two stiff whiskies, one quickly after the other. But neither the shower nor the whiskies had done anything to dent this soiled feeling I had nor lessen the feeling of guilt that I had betrayed Nina who was slaving all day to keep us going.

I walked slowly up the path from the garage, took out my key and opened the front door. The clock in the hall told me it was ten minutes after eleven o'clock. From the lounge, I could hear Renick's voice and Nina's sudden laugh.

I stood hesitating.

Renick and I had been close friends for twenty years. We had gone to school together. He had been a good, straight cop, and now he was the D.A.'s special officer, a position of importance in this city, carrying a good salary. If this kidnapping idea turned sour, he would be the first to be involved in the investigation, and I knew he was no fool. He was one of the brightest and shrewdest investigators of the whole bunch. In my newspaper work I had met them all: Renick topped the lot. If he handled the investigation I could be in trouble.

I braced myself, crossed to the lounge door and pushed it open.

Nina was working on a large garden pot that stood on her work bench. Renick lounged in an armchair, watching her, a cigarette burning between his fingers.

As soon as Nina saw me, she dropped her paint brush and ran over to me. She slid her arms around my neck and kissed me. The touch of her lips against mine gave me a sick

49

feeling. I was still remembering Odette's hot, animal caresses. I pushed her away gently and with my arm around her, I forced a smile as Renick got to his feet.

'Hello there, John,' I said and shook hands. 'You're a stranger.'

Once a cop, always a cop. I could see by his steady, puzzled stare, he knew something was wrong. He gripped my hand and his grin was as lop-sided as mine.

'That's not my fault, Harry,' he said. 'I've been in Washington for the past month. I've only just got back. How are you? I hear you have a job.'

'Well, call it that,' I said. 'It's better than nothing.'

I dropped into a lounging chair. Nina sat on the arm, her hand on mine and Renick went back to his chair. The searching, probing stare was still there.

'Look, Harry,' he said, 'you can't go on like this. You've got to get settled. I think I can swing this thing with Meadows if you want it.'

I stared at him.

'Meadows? Swing what?'

'My boss,' Renick said. 'I told you: I spoke to him about you. We need a good Public Relations man: you're hand-made for the job.'

'Am I? Well, I don't think so,' I said. After what those jerks did to me, I wouldn't work for the City for any money.'

Nina's grip tightened on my hand.

'Be reasonable, Harry, for heaven's sake!' Renick said

'The old gang's gone. This is a big opportunity. We don't know what it'll pay yet, but it'll be good money. Meadows knows all about your case and your reputation as a newspaper man. If we can get a grant for the salary, and we're pretty sure we can, the job's yours.'

It crossed my mind that here was my chance to drop this kidnapping stunt and get down to a solid job of work. I hesitated, thinking of the fifty thousand dollars. With that amount of money behind me, I could be my own boss.

'I'll think about it,' I said. 'Maybe the old gang has gone, but I'm still not sold about working for the City. Anyway, I'll think about it.'

50

'But don't you think you should take it?' Nina said anxiously. 'It's work you like and you. . .'

'I said I'd think about it,' I said curtly.

Renick looked disappointed.

'Well, all right. Of course it's not certain, we'll get a grant, but if we do, we'll want a quick decision. There are a couple of other guys after the job already.'

'There always are,' I said, 'Thanks, John, for the offer. I'll let you know.'

He gave a helpless little shrug, then got to his feet.

'Okay. I must get moving. I just dropped in to tell you. You give me a call.'

When he had gone, Nina said, 'You're not going to turn this offer down, are you, Harry? You must see.. .' 'I'm going to think about it. Come on, let's go to bed.' She put her hand on my arm as she said, 'If they get the grant, I want you to take this job. We can't go on much longer like this. You must get settled.'

'Will you let me handle my own life?' I said sharply. 'I said I would think about it, and that's what I'm going to do.'

I went into the bedroom, and after putting the tape I had recorded into a drawer, I got undressed.

I could hear Nina moving about the kitchen, clearing up. I got into bed.

Again I balanced this offer of Renick's against Rhea's fifty thousand dollars. Maybe this grant wouldn't jell. Maybe something would turn sour with the kidnapping. I would have to wait and see. Maybe with any luck I might land both Renick's offer and Rhea's money.

Nina came in. I pretended to be half asleep. I watched her undress through half closed eyes. She got into bed beside me and turned off the light. When she moved close to me, I shifted away. I felt such a heel, I couldn't bear to have her touch me.

The next day was Thursday. Nina wanted the car as she had some pots to take down to the shop. There was nothing for me to do, so I hung around the bungalow and I kept thinking of Odette.

By now my first feeling of guilt had worn off. I had told myself as I had driven from the cabin last night that when we met again, there would be no repetition of what had happened. This was my first slip; there wasn't going to be another, but this morning, as I mooned around the bungalow. I found myself thinking differently.

I was now telling myself it couldn't possibly hurt Nina if I again made love to Odette. The time to have stopped was the first time; the second time made no difference. Once you did it, you had done it. I even began to imagine I had enjoyed Odette's savage, primitive embrace, and as the hours dragged by, I found myself waiting impatiently for tomorrow night.

Later in the day I went to the bank and lodged the tape with the other one, then I went to the beach cabin and spent the rest of the day swimming and sitting in the sun, my mind gradually becoming obsessed with Odette.

The following morning, as we were finishing breakfast, Nina said, 'Have you decided about John's offer?'

'Not yet,' I said, 'but I'm considering it.'

She stared steadily at me and I had to shift my eyes.

'Well, while you are making up your mind,' she said, 'there are three bills that must be paid. I haven't the money.' She dropped the bills on to the table. 'The garage man won't let us have any more gas until we have settled his account. The electricity bill must be paid or we'll be without light. The grocery bill must be settled. They won't give us any more credit.'

I still had sixty dollars left from the hundred Rhea had paid me. At least I could take care of the grocery and the electricity bills.

'I'll fix these,' I said. 'The garage man must wait. Have we any gas?'

'About half a tank.'

'We'd better use the bus whenever we can.' 'I have four pots to deliver tomorrow I can't use the bus.'

There was a sharp note of exasperation in her voice I had never heard before. I looked at her. She faced me, her dark eyes unhappy and angry. The prick of conscience made me angry too.

'I didn't say you couldn't use the car,' I said. 'I just said when we could we'd better use the bus.'

'I heard you.'

'All right then.'

She hesitated. I could see she wanted to say something further, but instead, she turned and left the room.

I felt bad. This was the nearest we had ever come to a quarrel. I left the bungalow and walked to the bus stop. I settled the two bills: that left me with fifteen dollars. At the end of the week Bill Holden would want the rent for the cabin, but with any luck, I would be worth fifty thousand by then.

I spent the rest of the day at the beach cabin, swimming, lounging in the sun and watching the clock, counting the minutes to the time when Odette would come up the veranda steps.

Again the beach became, deserted soon after half past eight. I was now sitting on the veranda, as tense as any schoolboy waiting for his first date.

A little after nine o'clock, she came out of the darkness. As soon as I caught sight of her, I was out of my chair, stupidly excited, my heart thumping, and as she came up the steps, I caught hold of her, my hands gripping her arms, pulling her to me.

Then I got a shock.

She put her hands on my chest and gave me a hard shove, sending me backwards.

'Keep your paws to yourself,' she said in a cold, flat voice. When I want you to paw me, I'll tell you,' and she walked past me into the cabin.

I felt as if I had come under a douche of icy water. I felt suddenly deflated and horribly cheap. After a moment's hesitation, I followed her into the cabin and shut the door.

She was wearing powder blue slacks and a white pleated shirt. Her black hair was caught back by a white bandeau. She looked very desirable as she curled herself up on the settee.

'You should never jump to conclusions, little man,' she said and smiled. 'You mustn't ever take any woman for granted. You amused me the other night, but you don't amuse me tonight.'

This was my moment of truth. I could have killed her. I could have taken her by force, but those words put a picture of myself in a frame. They were needles, pricking a balloon.

53

I sat down. With an unsteady hand, I lit a cigarette.

'I'm glad I'm not your father,' I said. 'That's one thing I'm really glad about.'

She giggled, drawing smoke down into her lungs and expelling it through her pinched nostrils.

'Why bring my father into it? You're just mad at me because I'm not the easy toy you thought I was. They all say the same: stupid, unsuccessful men with a sex itch.' She smoothed down her dark hair as she stared mockingly at me. 'Now we have got over all that, shall we talk business?'

I hated her then more than I thought it possible to hate anyone.

I had trouble in opening my briefcase and taking out the papers on which I had written my questionnaire. My hands shook so badly, the papers made a rustling noise.

'I'll ask the questions,' I said, my voice scarcely under control, 'you give me the answers.'

'You don't have to get upset, little man,' she said. 'You're being very well paid.'

'Shut up!' I snarled at her. 'I don't want any of your cheap remarks,' then I began to fire questions at her. 'Why did she go to the Pirates' Cabin?' 'What was the room like in which she was imprisoned?' What was the woman like who fed her?' 'Did she see anyone else besides this woman while she was in the farmhouse?' and so on and so on.

Her answers were slick and smooth. Not once did she hesitate nor make a mistake.

We kept at it for over two hours. During those hours of intensive questioning, she never once put a foot wrong.

Finally, I said, 'You'll do. Just so long as you don't alter the story and you watch out for traps, you'll do.'

She gave me a small, mocking smile.

'I'll watch out for traps... Harry.'

I got to my feet.

'Well, okay, then we're ready for Saturday. I'll be at the Pirates' Cabin at nine-fifteen. You know what to do.'

She uncurled herself off the settee and stood up.

'Yes, I know what to do.'

We looked at each other, then her expression softened, and smiling, she moved towards me, that thing in her eyes.

'Poor little man,' she said. 'Paw me if you want to. I don't really mind.'

I waited until she was in range, then I slapped her face, hard. Her head jerked to one side. Then I slapped her again.

She stepped back, her hands going to her flaming cheeks, staring at me, her slate eyes glittering.

'You stinker!' she said shrilly. 'I'll remember that! You rotten stinker!'

'Get out!' I said. 'Before I hit him again!'

She moved to the door, swinging her neat hips. At the door she paused and turned to stare at me.

'I'm glad I'm not your wife,' she said. 'That's one thing I'm glad about,' then she suddenly giggled and turning, ran out into the moonlight and scampered away across the hard, damp sand.

I felt such a heel, I could have cut my throat.

CHAPTER FIVE

I

WHEN I got up on Saturday morning, there was a hint of rain in the air. I was nervous and uneasy. All my doubts about this job came crowding up out of my subconscious. It was only the thought of the money that stiffened my jittery nerves.

'I'll be late tonight,' I told Nina who was preparing breakfast. 'This is the last night of the traffic count.' She looked anxious at me.

'Will you be seeing John today?'

'I'll see him on Monday. If he had any news for me he would have telephoned.'

She hesitated, then asked, 'Are you going to take the job, Harry?'

'I think so. A lot depends on what they will pay.'

'John said the salary would be good.' She smiled at me. 'I'm so glad. You really have been worrying me.'

'I've been worrying myself,' I said lightly. 'I'm taking the car tonight. les going to rain.'

'There's very little gas, Harry.'

'That's okay. I'll fix it.'

Later, I went down to the beach cabin. I had just got into my swim trunks when Bill Holden appeared in the doorway.

'Hello there, Mr. Barber,' he said. 'Are you keeping the cabin on for another week?'

'I guess so,' I said. 'Maybe not for the whole week but at least until Thursday.

'Would you like to settle for this week?'

'I'll settle tomorrow. I've left my wallet at home.'

'That's okay, Mr. Barber — tomorrow's fine.'

I stared out at the grey, heavy sky.

'Looks like rain. I guess I'll have a swim before it.' Holden said he thought it would hold off until later, but he was wrong. I had just come in from the swim when the rain started.

I settled down in the cabin with a paper-back, The beach was now deserted. That suited me. I hoped the rain would go on all day.

Around one o'clock, I went over to the restaurant which was empty and ate a hamburger and drank a beer, then I returned to the cabin. As I pushed open the door, the telephone bell rang.

It was Rhea on the line.

'Is everything arranged?' she asked. There was an anxious note in her voice.

'On my side, it's arranged,' I said. 'I'm ready to go. Everything now depends on Odette.'

'You can depend on her.'

'Well, fine. Then at eight-forty-five, I'll start things moving.'

'I'll telephone you tomorrow at eleven o'clock.'

'I want some money,' I said. 'I have to pay for the rent of this cabin. Maybe it would be better if you came down here tomorrow morning. I'll be here.'

'I'll do that,' she said and hung up.

I remained in the cabin for the rest of the day. The rain beat down on the roof. The sea turned slate grey. I tried to concentrate on the paper-back, but it was impossible.

Finally, I got up and prowled up and down and smoked endless cigarettes, watching the time and waiting, waiting and waiting.

When at last the hands of my wrist watch showed eight-thirty, I left the cabin and ran across the wet sand to the Packard. It was still raining, but more lightly. I drove to a drug store in the main street of Palm City. By the time I had parked and had walked through the drizzle to the drug store, it was close on eight-forty-five.

I called Malroux's residence.

Almost immediately the call was answered.

'Mr. Malroux's residence,' an English voice announced. 'Who is this, please?'

'I want Miss Malroux,' I said. 'This is Jerry. Williams.'

'Will you hold the line, Mr. Williams? I'll see if Miss Malroux is available.'

I held the line, aware that I was breathing over-fast.

There was a longish delay, then Odette's voice said brightly, 'Hello?'

'Is anyone listening?'

'No. It's all right. Hello, Harry.' There was a caress in her voice. 'You're the only man who has ever dared to hit me. You are quite a character.'

'I know. Watch it I don't hit you again. You know what to do? I'll be at the Pirates' Cabin in twenty minutes. The Packard will be parked on the far right-hand side of the parking lot. The dress will be on the back seat. You haven't forgotten any of the details?'

'I haven't forgotten.'

'Then get moving. I'll be waiting for you,' and I hung up.

It took me a quarter of an hour, driving fast to reach the Pirates' Cabin. The parking lot was pretty full, but I managed to park the Packard where I had told her it would be. There was no parking attendant and that suited me. Someone was playing a squeeze-box and singing. I could see through the windows that the bar was crowded.

I sat in the Packard and waited. I was pretty tense. Every car that came into the park made me stiffen., At twenty-five

57

minutes after nine, I saw a white T.R.3 slide through the gates and park within twenty yards of my car.

Odette climbed out. She was wearing a white plastic mack over a scarlet dress. She paused beside the T.R.3 and looked in my direction.

I leaned out of the Packard and waved to her. The thin drizzle of rain was now becoming heavier. She waved back, and then walked quickly to the restaurant and entered the bar.

I got out of the Packard and crossed over to her car. There was a suitcase lying on the passenger's seat. I looked to right and left, satisfied myself no one was watching me, then took the suitcase over to the Packard.

Through the bar windows I could see Odette. She was speaking to the barman. He shook his head at her and she moved away from the bar and out of my sight.

I looked at my wrist watch. The plane to Los Angeles left at ten-thirty. We had plenty of time. I had made her reservation by telephone in the name of Ann Harcourt. I had told the clerk she would pick up and pay for her ticket at the airport. I had also telephoned and reserved a room at a small hotel in Los Angeles that I had once stayed at. It was quiet, and away from the centre of the town, I felt sure she would be all right there.

I saw Odette come out of the bar. My heart skipped a beat when I saw she wasn't alone: there was a man with her.

She began to walk towards the Packard. The man caught hold of her arm, pulling her back. I couldn't see much of him. He was short and fat, and he was wearing a light coloured suit.

'Come on, baby,' he said in a loud, wheedling voice, 'let's have a party. I'm on my own: you're on your own; let's be lonely together.'

'Get away from me!' Odette said. 'Take your hands off me!' She sounded scared.

'Aw come on, baby. Let's have some fun together.'

If she couldn't handle him, we were in trouble. I didn't dare show myself. He might not be as drunk as he seemed. If things turned sour, he might remember me.

'Get away from me!' Odette repeated and she started once more towards the Packard. The drunk hesitated, then came after her.

I moved around to the off-side of the car. I wanted to yell to her to keep away from the Packard. He might remember the car, but she kept coming.

The drunk staggered after her, caught hold of her arm and swung her around.

'Hey! Don't get snooty with me baby. Come on back. I'll buy you a drink.'

She slapped his face. The sound her hand made as it contacted his face was a minor explosion.

'Okay, so you're tough,' the drunk snarled and grabbing her, he tried to kiss her.

I had to do something now. She was struggling, but I could see he was too strong for her. She had enough sense not to cry out.

In the glove compartment of the Packard I always kept a heavy flashlight. I grabbed hold of it. It was a foot long and made a good club.

It was pretty dark, and we were away from the single spotlight above the gates. I circled around so I could come up behind him. I was so jittery, my breath was whistling through my clenched teeth.

As I came up, Odette managed to break free. The drunk became aware of me and spun around.

I slammed him over the head with the flashlight, driving him to his knees. I heard Odette catch her breath in a strangled scream.

Cursing, the drunk made a grab at me, but I hit him again: this time much harder, and with a grunt, he spread out, face down at my feet.

'Take my car!' I said to Odette. 'Get going! I'll follow in your car!'

'Have you hurt him?' She was staring down at the drunk, her hands to her face.

'Get going!'

I ran over to the T.R.3, got in and started the engine. If anyone came out of the restaurant and found this guy lying in full view, we would be in a hell of a jam.

As I reversed the little car, I heard the Packard start up. I let her drive out of the parking lot, then I followed her.

59

She had enough sense to head for the beach road. After we had driven a mile or so, I overtook her and signalled her to stop.

The road was deserted. The rain was now streaming down. I got out of her car and ran back to where she had stopped the Packard.

'Get changed!' I said. 'Then follow me to Lone Bay car park. Hurry!'

'Did you hurt him badly?' she asked as she reached into the back of the car for the dress.

'Forget it! Never mind about him! Get changed! Time's running out.'

I ran back to the T.R.3 and got in. I sat there, sweating and watching the road, praying no stray car would come along and spot us.

After about five minutes — the time seemed an eternity — I heard her tap the horn and I looked back. She waved to me. I started the little car and drove fast to Lone Bay.

She followed.

I kept looking at my wrist watch. We still had plenty of time to reach the airport. It was two miles beyond Lone Bay. I kept thinking of the drunk, wondering if I had hit him too hard. But now it was over, I realized perhaps it hadn't been such a bad thing to have happened. If Odette ever had to face up to a police investigation, it would strengthen her story: just so long as I hadn't hit him too hard or he hadn't one of the egg shell skulls one is always reading about.

Lone Bay car park served a colony of bungalows. The residents used the park as a permanent parking place, and it was always full of cars. I felt pretty confident the T.R.3 could be left there without anyone spotting it. As I approached the park, I signalled to Odette to stop, then I swung the sports car into the park.

There was a narrow aisle between the parked cars, and I drove slowly down this aisle, my headlights on, looking for a vacant place.

Then suddenly, without warning, a car backed out into the aisle. It hadn't its lights on. It came out fast and I hadn't a chance to avoid it. It's rear bumper thudded into my off-wing, and there was a grinding sound of crushed metal.

For a brief moment, I sat paralysed. This was the one thing I hadn't thought of: an accident. This stupid ape would want my name and address: he would take the number of the car and it would immediately be traced to Odette. What was I doing — driving her car?

While I sat there in a panic that stood my hair on ends, the driver got out of the car.

It was fortunately dark in the parking lot. As he came up to me, I turned off my headlights. I could see he was a small man with a bald head, but I couldn't see much of his features and that meant he couldn't see much of mine.

'I'm sorry, mister,' he said in a shaking voice. 'I didn't see you coming. It's my fault. I'm entirely to blame.'

A large woman got out of the car. She opened an umbrella and joined the little man.

'It wasn't your fault, Herbert!' she said angrily. 'He shouldn't have sneaked up like that. Don't you admit anything. It was an accident.'

'Get your car forward,' I said. 'You've locked my front wing.'

'Don't you move the car, Herbert,' the woman said. 'We'll get a policeman.'

Cold sweat was running down my back.

'You heard what I said!' I bawled at the little man. 'Get your goddam car forward!'

'Don't you speak to my husband like that!' The woman exclaimed. She was staring hard at me. 'This is your fault, young man! You don't intimidate me!'

Time was running out. I didn't dare exchange names and addresses with these two. I did the only thing left to me. I engaged gear, twisted the steering wheel and trod down hard on the gas.

As the little car jumped forward, there was a grinding noise and the other man's bumper came away. Part of my wing came away too. I kept going as I heard the woman scream: 'Take his number, Herbert!'

I drove fast to the far end of the parking lot, found an empty space, swung the car into and jumped out. I was wearing gloves so I didn't have to stop to wipe off the steering wheel. I looked back down the aisle.

The woman was staring after me. The little man was trying to lift the fallen bumper.

There was an exit just ahead of me. I ran for it. Would they go to the police? It was his fault. There was just a chance they would let it go. If they didn't, the T.R.3 would be traced to Odette. The police would want to know who the man was driving the car.

As I sprinted towards the waiting Packard, I realized with a sudden sinking feeling of fear, that my highly organized arrangements weren't working the way I had planned them to work.

First the drunk: now this car accident.

What else was going to go wrong with this zany idea of mine?

II

The next morning I was woken out of a heavy sleep by the sound of the telephone bell ringing.

I sat up in bed with a start, only half awake, and I looked at the bedside clock. The time was twenty minutes to eight.

I could hear Nina talking to someone, and I forced myself to relax back on my pillow. I reached for a pack of cigarettes on the night table.

As I lit the cigarette, my mind jumped to the events of the previous night. I had seen Odette off at the airport. I hadn't told her about the car accident. There was no point in upsetting her nerves. It was bad enough for my nerves to be upset without involving hers. She had gone off happily enough, having got over the shock of the drunk. She had the resilience of youth. During the drive to the airport, I had assured her I hadn't hurt the guy and once she was convinced, she was able to dismiss him from her mind. But I couldn't: nor could I dismiss from my mind the car accident.

During the drive from the airport, I tried to convince myself it was going to work out all right. The drunk who I had knocked on the head, knowing he had tried to assault Odette, was pretty certain to keep his mouth shut. The man and the women who owned the car that had crashed into the T.R.3

might not tell the police, knowing it was their fault that the car had backed into mine.

When I had reached Palm City I had gone to a bar in a quiet street. I had had a couple of drinks. The bar was crowded with people sheltering from the rain. No one paid any attention to me.

I shut myself in a pay booth and had called Malroux's telephone number.

While I waited, listening to the thump-thump-thump of my heart, I wondered if Odette had safely reached her hotel. After a delay, I heard the butler's voice.

'Give me Mr. Malroux,' I said, making my voice sound hard and curt. 'I have a message from his daughter.'

'Who is this, please.

I fairly yelled at him: 'Do what I say! Tell Malroux to come to the phone!'

'Will you hold on?'

There was a shocked note in the man's voice.

I heard him lay down the receiver. I waited, feeling sweat on my face. I kept looking through the glass panel of the booth at the crowded bar. No one looked my way.

Then a quiet voice said in my ear, 'This is Malroux.

Who is calling?'

Well, at least Rhea hadn't been bluffing. She had said she would make him come to the phone and he had come.

'Listen carefully, pal,' I said speaking slowly so he couldn't miss a word. 'We've kidnapped your daughter. We want five hundred thousand bucks. Do you hear me? Five hundred grand and in small bills. If you don't pay up you won't see her again — that's a promise. You're not to call in the cops and no tricks — understand? This is a snatch pal. If you want to see your daughter again, you'll do as I'm telling you.'

There was a moment's pause, then the quiet voice said, 'I understand. I will pay, of course. How do I deliver the money and how is my daughter to be returned?'

He sounded as calm and as unruffled as a politician presiding over a tea party.

'I'll telephone you Monday,' I said. 'How soon can you get the money? The sooner you get it the better for your daughter.'

63

'I'll have it ready tomorrow.'

'Tomorrow's Sunday'

'I'll have it ready tomorrow.'

'Okay. I'll phone you Monday morning. You'll get instructions where to deliver it, and remember, one word to the cops, any tricks and you won't see the kid again. You'll find her in a ditch, but not before we've had some fun with her.'

I replaced the receiver and went out to the Packard.

I didn't feel proud of myself, but this was a job. The money involved was too big to worry about pride. I was glad to find Nina asleep. I didn't get much sleep that night. It seemed I had barely dozed off when the telephone bell woke me.

I now listened intently to the sound of Nina's voice as she talked to the caller.

When I heard her quick steps coming down the passage, I braced myself.

The bedroom door opened.

'Harry ... it's John. He wants to talk to you. He says it's urgent.'

I threw off the sheet and slipped on the dressing-gown she held for me.

'What's so urgent?' I said. 'Did he tell you?'

'No. He's asking for you.'

'Okay. I'll talk to him.'

I went into the lounge and picked up the telephone receiver.

'John? This is Harry.'

'Hello there, boy,' John said. His voice sounded excited. 'Now listen: I've got this job fixed for you, and you could be right into something that could be a sensation. I want you to come down here right away. I'm calling from the D.A.'s office. Just to make it sweet for you, they're going to offer you a hundred and fifty and expenses. But never mind that. The point is we can use you, Harry, and fast. We could have something on our hands that'll start a prairie fire. You've heard of Felix Malroux: the French millionaire? It looks as if his daughter has been kidnapped. If she has — brother! Will this

64

be something! It's just the set-up you can handle. Come, down here right away. The D.A. will want to talk to you.'

I felt icy fingers closing over my heart.

'Now, wait a minute,' I said my voice unsteady, 'I didn't say I'd work for the Administration.'

'For the love of Mike, Harry!' Renick's voice shot up half an octave. 'If this turns out to be what I think it is, it's going to be the biggest goddamn thing that's ever hit Mt Palm City. Don't you want to be in on it?'

I was aware that Nina was standing in the doorway, looking at me. My hand was so slippery with sweat I had trouble holding the receiver. So the lid had already come off this thing. *It looks as if his daughter has been kidnapped.* If I worked with the D.A., at least I would know what the moves were. I hesitated for about three seconds, then I said, 'I'm on my way, John.'

'Fine ... fine ... and hurry,' Renick said. 'I'll be waiting for you.'

I put down the receiver.

'What is it, Harry?' Nina asked.

'I don't know. He's excited about something. He didn't say. He wants me down at the D.A.s' office. They're paying a hundred and fifty and I'm not turning that
down.'

'Oh Harry!' She threw her arms around me. 'I'm so glad. A hundred and fifty l' She kissed me. 'I knew it would be all right for you. I knew it!'

I wasn't in the mood for love. I patted her and then pushed her away.

'I've got to get down there fast.'

I went into the bedroom and threw on my clothes. My heart was hammering so hard I had trouble with my breathing. So Rhea had been too confident. Malroux had told the police. Well, I had lost out. I wasn't going to make fifty thousand dollars, but at least, I had a hundred and fifty dollars a week job.

I paused as I knotted my tie.

But had I the job?

If the police found out I was mixed up in this faked

65

kidnapping, I wouldn't hold the job for five minutes. Maybe those two tapes would save me from being prosecuted, but they wouldn't save the job.

I got down to the D.A.'s office a few minutes after nine o'clock. A girl took me to Renick's office.

'Come on in, Harry,' he said, getting up from behind a massive desk. He gripped my hand. 'I'm glad you've decided to throw in with us. You won't regret it. The D.A. is on his way now. He should be here any minute.'

I sat on the arm of a lounging chair and took the cigarette he offered me.

'What's all the excitement about John?' I said, trying to sound casual. 'What's this about Malroux's daughter?' There was a tap on the door and a girl looked in. 'Mr. Meadows is here now, Mr. Renick.'

Renick stood up.

'Let's talk to Meadows,' he said.

As we walked down the long passage, Renick went on, 'Watch your step with him. He's a good guy, but a little touchy. He knows all about you and he admires your work and also the way you came out of that mess. You deliver the goods, and you'll have no trouble with him.' He paused outside a door, rapped and entered.

A thick-set man with chalk white hair was standing by the window, lighting a cigar. He glanced around. His small, piercing blue eyes swept over me. He was around fifty: his red fleshy face, jutting chin and his thin hard mouth gave me an immediate impression of ruthless efficiency.

'This is Harry Barber,' Renick said. 'He's on the staff from this morning.'

Meadows pushed out a cold, hard hand.

'Glad to hear it,' he said. 'I've heard about you, Barber: what I've heard is good.'

I shook hands with him.

Blowing a cloud of smoke from between his thin lips, Meadows walked over to his desk and sat down. He waved Renick and myself to chairs.

'You've spoilt my week-end,' he said to Renick. 'I was planning to take the wife and kids for a picnic. What's all this about?'

66

Renick dropped into a chair and crossed his long legs.

'Could be we have a kidnapping on our hands, sir,' he said. 'I thought you would want to be in on it from the start. Early this morning, I had a telephone call from Masters, the manager of the Californian and Los Angeles Bank.' He looked, over at me. 'We have an arrangement with all the banks to report sudden withdrawals of any large sums of money if the circumstances seem urgent and unusual. From experience, we have learned that such withdrawals usually mean they are for ransom demands.'

I took out my handkerchief and wiped my sweating face. This was something I hadn't known and hadn't even suspected.

'Masters said he had just had a telephone call from Malroux telling him to open up the bank and have ready for him five hundred thousand dollars. This is Sunday of course, and Masters tried to persuade Malroux to wait until tomorrow, but Malroux, who is the bank's best client, said he must have the money right away. This seemed to conform to the arrangement between Masters and us, so he telephoned.'

Meadows scratched his chin.

'Maybe Malroux is swinging a business deal involving cash.'

'That's what I thought, and I decided to check.' Renick looked over at me. 'As you should know, Harry, what usually happens in a kidnapping case is the parents of the kidnapped child are so scared that something will happen to their child that they pay up at once without consulting us. They seldom give us the chance to mark the money or set a trap for the kidnappers. Then when the child isn't returned, they come running to us and expect us to find it. I'm blaming no one for not coming to us: a kidnapper is the most vicious type of criminal we know. He always warns his victim if he goes to the police the child will be murdered, but by not coming to us, they put us in a bad position to get moving. Hence this idea of getting bank managers to co-operate secretly. We don't, of course, act on the information — we can't but at least we are geared and ready to go into action when the parents do ask for help.'

'What makes you think the girl has been kidnapped?' I asked, feeling I should say something.

67

'She's missing,' Renick returned. 'Malroux's chauffeur is an ex-cop. When Malroux came to live here, he wanted a bodyguard. A man with his wealth is constantly being pestered by cranks. He asked us to recommend a thoroughly experienced man who could act as his chauffeur and keep him clear of trouble. O'Reilly wanted a change. He was a good cop, and he was sick of the way things were being run at that time. He took the job. I've had a word with him. He tells me Odette Malroux, the daughter, had a date last night to go to the movies with a girl friend. Odette didn't turn up at the movies and O'Reilly says she didn't come home last night.'

'How does he know she didn't go to the movies?' Meadows demanded.

'The girl friend telephoned and O'Reilly took the message. 'Malroux hasn't asked for our help?'

'No.' Renick got to his feet and began to wander around the office. 'I have a man watching the bank. He'll report to me as soon as Malroux gets the money.' 'Is Masters recording the numbers of the bills?' Renick made a grimace.

'I don't think so. Recording small bills worth five hundred thousand would take a hell of a time.'

'What about this girl? Know anything about her? She couldn't have run off to get married?'

'Then why does Malroux want all this money?'

'Blackmail?'

Renick shrugged.

'I doubt it: more like kidnapping. As for the girl, she is about twenty and pretty. She gets around and has more freedom than is good for her. She's had a number of speeding raps. We have her fingerprints and there are plenty of photographs we can get from the Press.'

Meadows brooded for a long moment, then he said, 'If this is kidnapping, it is going to be a sensation. We're going to be right in the limelight.' He looked over at me. 'This is where you come in, Barber. It'll be your job to handle the Press, and believe you me, every newspaper man in the country will come storming down here.' He pointed a fat finger at me. 'I like publicity, Barber, so long as it is good publicity. Understand? It's your job to see I get it. It's your job to see I don't get panned.

That's what we are paying you for. It's your job to put Palm City on the map. A kidnapping like this is just the thing to put a town on the, map. You have a very responsible job, Barber: that's why we picked you.

'I understand, sir.' I said.

Meadows turned to Renick who was still prowling around the office.

'Is her car missing?'

'Yes. It's a white T.R.3. O'Reilly gave me the number.'

Can't do any harm to look for it. Tell the boys to find it. There's not much else we can do until Malroux calls us in. I'll talk to the Police Commissioner. How about talking to the Federal boys. They'll come into this automatically.'

'I'll do that, sir.'

'Okay, let's get going.' He looked over at me. 'We don't want you for the moment, Barber. You might, as well enjoy your Sunday. Give Renick a call every two hours just in case something breaks. Right?'

I got to my feet.

'Sure.' I hesitated, then went on, 'Just an idea, sir. Couldn't we watch Malroux when he's got the money? Couldn't we follow him if he delivers the money some place?'

Meadows shook his head.

'That's one thing we're not going to do,' he said. 'We don't do a damn thing until he asks us to. Suppose we followed him, suppose we were spotted by the kidnappers and they flipped their lids and killed the girl: what would happen to me? No, I'm not taking that risk. We don't do a thing until Malroux calls us in.'

Here then was a chance, I thought as I nodded.

'I see that. Well, I'll call you, John, at eleven-thirty.'

As I started across to the door, Meadows reached for the telephone. John was already on the other one.

I closed the door and went down the passage to my eleven o'clock rendezvous with Rhea Malroux.

CHAPTER SIX

I

As I drove to the beach cabin, it began to rain. There was
a chilly wind and the sea was grey and rough: not a day to
spend on the beach, and there was no one in sight as I drove
into Bill Holden's parking lot.

I went to the cabin, shut myself in and put a call through
to the Regent Hotel, Los Angeles.

After a few minutes' delay, I was speaking to Odette. 'This
is Harry,' I said. 'Listen carefully: we could be in trouble. I can't
talk over an open line, but whatever you do, stay in your room.
I'll be phoning you again. I may want you back tomorrow.'

I heard her catch her breath.

'Is that man — the drunk?'

'No. It's worse than that. The people I thought would come
into this later are already in it. Do you understand?'

'What are we going to do?'

'It may still work. If I think it won't, I'll call you again
tonight. For now, keep out of sight and stay in your room.'

'But what's happening?' There was a touch of panic in her
voice. 'Can't you tell me?'

'Not over an open line. Just stay where you are and don't
go out. I'll call you tonight,' and I hung up.

I felt sorry for her, but I didn't dare talk. I didn't know if
the girl on the hotel switchboard was listening in.

I went to the window and looked out. The heavy rain was
making patterns on the sand. The beach looked forlorn and
empty. I lit a cigarette and began to prowl around the room.

At least Malroux hadn't called in the police so far, but if
the police found the T.R.3 with its crushed wing, they would
have the excuse to call on him, and then he might admit his
daughter was missing.

I saw Rhea coming across the beach. She was wearing a
black raincoat, and she was sheltering under an umbrella. If
Holden caught sight of her, he couldn't possibly recognize her
as she held the umbrella so it hid her face.

I opened the door as she came up the steps.

70

'He's collecting the money from the bank now,' she said as she folded the umbrella and shook it before coming in. 'I told him I was going to church to pray for Odette.'

I am not a religious man, but that cold-blooded statement gave me a feeling of disgust and an acute dislike for her.

'When do you plan to correct the money?' she asked as I took her raincoat. She went over to a lounging chair and sat down.

'I'm not all that sure we're going to get it,' I said.

She stiffened, her eyes hardening.

'What do you mean?'

'Maybe this will surprise you,' I said, putting the raincoat on the table and sitting down. 'Your husband's bank manager and his chauffeur have shot their mouths off. The police know already that Odette has been kidnapped.

If I had slapped her across her face, the effect of my words couldn't have been more electrifying.

'You're lying!' She jumped to her feet, her face chalk white and her eyes glittering. 'You've lost your nerve! You're scared to collect the money!'

'Do you think so?' Her frightened rage helped to steady my own feeling of panic. 'This morning, Mr. Masters, the manager of your husband's bank, called the District Attorney and told him your husband wanted five hundred thousand dollars in a hurry. It seems there is an arrangement now between bank managers and the police for the bank managers to inform the police when large sums are drawn from their customers' accounts in small bills, and in a hurry. The police automatically assume, until proved otherwise, this money is for a ransom note.'

'How do you know this?' she demanded shrilly.

I told her about my new job and how I had talked to the D.A.

'Renick has already talked to your chauffeur, O'Reilly,' I went on. 'Maybe you don't know, but O'Reilly is an ex-cop. He's told Renick that Odette didn't meet her girl friend last night, nor did she come home. The D.A. has put two and two together and has made four. He is sure Odette has been kidnapped, and he's standing by for the biggest sensation since the Lindberg case.'

71

Rhea put her hand to her throat and sat down abruptly. She was no longer beautiful. The expression of fear and frustrated fury was ugly to see.

'What are we going to do?' she said at last. She began to hammer the arm of her chair with her clenched fists. 'I must have the money!'

'I warned you, didn't I?' I said. 'I told you the police could come into this.'

'Never mind what you told me! What are we going to do?'

'You'd better hear the whole story, then maybe you can decide what you want to do.'

I gave her all the details. I told her about the drunk, the car accident and that the police were now looking for the T.R.3, and when they found it, they would come to her husband and ask questions.

She sat motionless, her hands clenched between her knees while she listened.

'Well, that's it,' I said. 'On the credit side, the, D.A. won't make a move unless your husband asks him to. They won't attempt to follow your husband when he goes out to deliver the money. Everything really depends on your husband. Will he tell the police Odette has been kidnapped when they question him about her car?' She drew in a long slow breath as she glared at me.

'So this is what you call efficiency!' she said furiously. 'Your clever little plan! Couldn't you have guessed she would have got involved with some drunk, going to a place like the Pirates' Cabin?'

I didn't say anything. I watched her, wondering just how good her nerve was.

There was a long pause, then she said, 'Well don't sit there, staring at me like a zombie. What are we going to, do?'

'That's, up to you,' I said. 'If you can persuade your husband not to tell the police, we can still go ahead, but I warn you when Odette gets back, the police are certain to question her about the car.'

'I must have the money!'

'If your husband doesn't talk to the police, I'll get it for you.

'He won't. After you telephoned, he said he wasn't calling

in the police. I didn't even have to persuade him. He is prepared to pay so long as he gets Odette back.'

'Well, if you're sure he won't talk, then we can still go ahead.'

'I'm sure.'

I looked at my wrist watch. The time was just eleven-thirty.

'I'll find out what's happening,' I said and reached for the telephone. I called Renick. When I got him, I asked, 'Anything breaking? Do you want me?'

'Nothing yet.' He sounded irritable. 'We haven't found her car. Malroux collected the money ten minutes ago. The Federal Agents are standing by. Give me a call around three o'clock. We may have the car by then.' I said I would do that and hung up.

Rhea stared at me. She was very tense.

'They haven't found the car yet. With any luck they won't find it,' I said. 'The next move is to get Odette's letter to your husband.' I took the letter from my pocket book. I had put the envelope in a plastic slip-case to guard against my fingerprints getting on the envelope. 'How do you get your mail?'

'There is a box at the gate.'

"When you go back, put this in the box. Make sure no one sees you do it. In this letter are the delivery instructions for tomorrow.' As she took the letter, I went on, 'Be careful how you handle it. You don't want your prints on the envelope. Use gloves when you take it out of the slipcase.'

She put the letter in her bag.

'So you're going ahead with this?' she said.

'That's what you are paying me for, isn't it? I think we can get away with it. At least, now I'm working for the other side, I'll know the moves. If it looks bad, I'll let you know, The set-up now is this: I'll call Odette and tell her to come back tomorrow night on the eleven o'clock plane.

She'll be here around one o'clock. She'll wait here. your husband is to drive along East Beach Road until he sees a flashing light. He will drop the briefcase as he passes the light. I should have the money by two-thirty. He, will drive on to Lone Bay, expecting to find Odette. You will come here, and I'll join, you two at two-forty-five. We will split up the money. Your husband, not finding Odette, will come home' You and Odette will be there, waiting for him. Your story will be that after he had gone, Odette just walked in. I've coached her in her story and she should be able to convince him. That's the set-up.' She thought for a long moment ' then she nodded.

'All right ... then tomorrow night at two-forty-five here.'

'Watch out for O'Reilly,' I said. 'Make sure he doesn't see you leave. This guy is a police spy. From now on, anything he spots, to do with this set-up, will go back to the D.A.: so watch out.'

She got to her feet

'I understand.'

'Fine. Now I want some money.' I said. 'I have to pay the rent of this cabin. Fifty will cover it.'

She gave me the money.

'Then tomorrow night...'

'That's it.' There was something about her manner that made me uneasy. I couldn't put my finger on it but it was there. 'You watch out for O'Reilly.'

She looked at me.

'You're sure you can handle this?'

'I wouldn't touch it if I wasn't sure.'

'I must have this money,' she said. 'I expect you to get it for me — I'm paying you enough.'

She moved to the door, opened it, put up her umbrella and walked down the steps into the rain.

I watched her move across the sodden sand to the car park.

When she had driven away, I walked under the shelter of the coverway that connected all the cabins to Bill Holden's office. I paid him the rent of the cabin.

'Is the work going okay, Mr. Barber?' he asked as gave me the receipt.

For a second or so, I stared at him, not knowing what he meant, then I remembered and gave him a fatuous grin.

'It's going fine,' I said. 'I'll need the cabin for one more night. Okay with you?'

'Anything you say, Mr. Barber.' He looked gloomily out of

his office window. 'I've never known such weather. It's ruining me. Look at it!'

'It'll clear up tomorrow,' I said. 'Cheer up! I've just paid you rent, haven't I?'

Leaving him, I returned to the cabin.

I hung around there until after two o'clock, then I ran through the rain to the snack bar across the way and had a sandwich lunch. When I got back to the cabin, I called Nina. I told her I didn't know when I would be back.

'The job's fixed, Harry?'

'The job's fixed,' I said. 'From now on, I'm fixed too. From now on, we've nothing to worry about.'

I wished I really believed that. I had plenty to worry about.

'That's wonderful. The note in her voice made me feel more of a heel. 'What did John want you for so urgently?'

'I'll tell you when I get back. I can't talk on the telephone.'

'I'll be waiting for you, Harry.'

'I'll be back as soon as I can.

At five minutes to three I called Renick.

There was a long delay before he came on the line.

'Harry? You're just in time.' His voice boomed in my car and he sounded excited. 'We've found the car! You know Lone Bay parking lot? Meet me there as soon as you can make it. I'm on my way now.'

With my throat suddenly dry and my heart thumping, I told him I was coming.

II

A large red-faced cop stood near the white T.R.3. Renick and a couple of detectives I didn't know were examining the car. It had stopped raining and the sun had come out.

As I came up, Renick said, 'Look at this, Harry. This is a bit of luck for us a bashed wing.'

'The two detectives glanced at me as I joined Renick by the car.

'Sure it's hers?' I said for something to say.

'The number and licence tag check. It's hers all right.' Turning to the two detectives, he went on, 'Check the car for prints and don't move it. When you're through, leave it as it is, and report back to me.'

Renick went on to me. 'I'm calling on Malroux. You come with me. This bashed wing gives me the chance to talk to him. We'll take your car. You can drop me off at headquarters after we have talked to him

I wished I could warn Rhea that we were coming, but there was no chance of that. It didn't take us ten-minutes to reach Malroux's residence.

The house was hidden behind high walls. As we drove up to the massive wooden gates, a broad-shouldered man in a dove grey uniform came out of a nearby lodge and looked inquiringly at us.

'Calling on Miss Malroux,' Renick said.

The man shook his head.

'She's not in.'

'Know where I can contact her?'

'I don't.'

'Then I guess I'll talk to Mr. Malroux.'

'Not without an appointment.'

'I'm Lieutenant Renick, City Police. It's an official call.'

The man look startled.

'I guess that's different. Stick around, Lieutenant.' He went into the lodge. Through the window I saw him using a telephone. There was a delay, then he came out and opened the gates.

'Go right ahead, Lieutenant.'

We drove up a sanded carriageway. On either side were lawns and flower beds. The massed effect of colour was impressive. We could see the house now. It was a low built Spanish styled house with terraces and an ornamental fountain. It looked what it was: the residence of one of the richest men in the world.

'Pretty lush,' Renick said as I parked the Packard on the tarmac apron beside the glittering Rolls. 'How would you like to own a joint like this?'

'I'd like it fine,' I said, following him up the steps. By now I was really worked up. Everything depended on what Malroux said. I felt the fifty thousand dollars that was coming to me hung in balance.

The butler was waiting for us by the front door. He was a fat, elderly man with a supercilious stare.

'Lieutenant Renick, City Police,' Renick said. 'I want to speak to Mr. Malroux.'

'If you will come this way.'

The butler led us across a patio where another fountain played, and out on to a large terrace that looked directly on the sea.

Rhea was in a lounging chair, leafing through a magazine. She was wearing sun goggles. She glanced up as we stepped on to the terrace.

A tall, thin man, very sun tanned, wearing a pair of white slacks and a blue and red sweat shirt sat in another lounging chair. This must be Malroux, I thought. He was handsome. His thick hair was steel grey. His steady blue eyes were very alive. It was impossible to believe that he was fatally ill.

'Mr. Malroux?' Renick said, pausing.

'That's right, Lieutenant. Sit down. What can I do for you?' The voice was impersonal and quiet. The steady blue eyes didn't encourage a spate of words.

'This is Harry Barber,' Renick said, waving to me. 'He works with me.' He didn't sit down. Malroux's voice and expression gave him the hint he wasn't wanted. 'I hoped to see Miss Malroux. I hear she isn't here sir.'

'That is right. What is it?'

'I'm sorry to bother you with this, Mr. Malroux,' Renick said in his smoothest manner, 'but I'm investigating a hit and run case. Late last night a woman was knocked down and fatally injured and the driver of the car didn't stop. We have been checking cars all day. We have found your daughter's car in Lone Bay parking lot. The car has a badly damaged wing. We would like to know how the accident happened.'

I watched Malroux and I sweated. Would he tell Renick his daughter had been kidnapped? His face was expressionless. He regarded Renick thoughtfully and with no apparent interest.

'If my daughter had knocked anyone down, she wouldn't run away. She is staying with friends I believe. I don't know

77

who they are. Young people, these days, don't tell their parents anything.'

I glanced at Rhea. She had gone back to leafing through her magazine. She appeared to be paying no attention to what was being said.

'When will she return?' Renick asked.

In a few days. When she does return, I will speak to her. I am quite sure she has nothing to do with this accident.'

'Can you explain, sir, why her car should be left at Lone Bay parking lot?'

Malroux moved restlessly.

'No. What my daughter does with her car is no concern of mine.' He reached out and picked up a book that was lying on the table. 'When my daughter returns, I will arrange for you to see her if it is still necessary. I am sure by then you will have traced the person responsible for the accident. I am satisfied my daughter has nothing to do with it. Good day to you, Lieutenant.'

'Well, that's that,' Renick said as we walked back to the Packard. 'He's a cool old bird, isn't he?'

I was feeling limp.

'We don't know for certain she has been kidnapped,' I said. 'He could have wanted that money for a business deal.'

Renick shook his head.

'I don't think so. Even a millionaire doesn't make a bank manager open his bank on a Sunday unless it is a life and death matter. I'm willing to bet she's been kidnapped. We'd better report to Meadows.'

The District Attorney was pacing his office and chewing a dead cigar when we walked in.

Renick told him about finding the car, about the bashed wing and of his interview with Malroux.

'He's not talking,' he concluded. 'I can't say I blame him. Do you think we should put a call out for the girl?'

Meadows throw his cigar into the trash basket.

'No. We'll wait. I'm not sticking my neck out. Malroux's got plenty of influence. If we move in now and make trouble for the girl, I'm the guy who'll hear about it. We'll wait.'

Renick shrugged.

'Okay, sir.' He turned to me. 'Keep near a telephone, Harry I may need you in a hurry. Are you going home?'

'Yes. If I go out I'll leave a telephone number with Nina where you can get me.'

'Do that.'

I drove home.

Nina was working in the lounge on a garden pot. She put down her paint brush as I came in.

'Darling ... I'm so excited.' She put her arms around me. 'Is it going to be all right?'

I swung her up in my arms and sat down with her on my lap'

'It's going to be all right. I'm working again and it's a job I'm going to like.'

She asked me why John had wanted me so urgently and on a Sunday. I told her about Malroux.

'John thinks the girl has been kidnapped, but I'm not worrying my brains until we know for certain. Personally, I think Malroux could have wanted the money for a big business deal.' I steered the conversation away from Malroux by asking her if she still planned to go on with her art work now I had a steady job.

'We can afford it if you want to drop it, I said.

'I think I'll go on. Anyway, until the end of the season.'

After dinner, I said I would go down to police headquarters to see if there was any news.

'I won't be long. I think it's an idea to show myself. I drove to the nearest drug store and called Odette.

'It's fixed for tomorrow night,' I said. 'It's going to work. I want you to catch the eleven o'clock plane back here. When you arrive take the bus to the terminus. You'll get there just after one. I'll be waiting for you. I'll take you to the cabin and leave you there. Then I'll collect you know what and come back.'

She said she understood. Her voice sounded anxious.

'You're sure it is going to be all right?'

'Yes... relax. I'll see you at the bus terminus at one o'clock, and I hung up' I then called police headquarters. The desk sergeant told me Renick had gone home. I guessed nothing had happened, so I went home myself.

The next morning, soon after nine, I went down to the District Attorney's office. It seemed odd to be starting a routine life again: odder to sit at a desk.

Renick's secretary gave me bunch of files. She said if I read through their contents. I would have a good picture of what was going on in the office. She said Renick would be in later in the day.

I started on the files. Renick came in soon after eleven. He sat on the edge of my desk and asked me how I liked the feel of work again.

'I like it fine,' I said. I waved my hand to the files. 'This is right up my street. Any news of the Malroux girl?' 'Nothing so far. I have a guy out at Lone Bay parking lot. If she turns up to take her car, he'll call me. There's nothing else I can do until Malroux calls us in. The Fedeal boys and the State police are all standing by.'

'If Malroux pays the ransom and the girl is returned, you may hear nothing further.'

'These days kidnappers don't usually return their victim. They are safer dead,' Renick said grimly. 'If she has been kidnapped I'll bet you he'll call us in.' He slid off the desk. 'Well, I've work to do. Anything you want — I'm right next door.'

When he had gone, I pushed aside the file I had been reading and lit a cigarette. By tomorrow morning, with any luck, I should be worth fifty thousand dollars. It was hard to believe. The money would be in small bills. I had already decided to rent a safe deposit and put the money there, drawing it from time to time, when I needed it. I would have to be careful. I couldn't suddenly alter my standard of life. Later, I could give out that I had made a killing on the Stock Market, but I would have to wait at least a year or so, if not longer.

Just as I was thinking of going to lunch, my office door jerked open and Renick came in. The excited expression on his face told me something had happened, and my heart turned a somersault.

'I think we've got a break!' he said. 'Come on down with me to police headquarters. I'll tell you about it on the way.' As we walked fast down the corridor to the elevator, he went on, 'Talk about luck! I was going through the routine police reports for Saturday night, and I turned up an item that could be something. A man was found unconscious in the car park at the Pirates' Cabin. Do you know it?'

My mouth turned so dry, I couldn't speak. I managed to give a grunt and nod.

'This guy had a pretty bad head wound. The barman called a cop. He told the cop this fellow had followed a girl into the car park. He said he had an idea the girl was Odette Malroux.'

'What makes him think that?' I asked huskily.

'She's a well-known character in Palm City. Her photos are always appearing in the Press. He was pretty sure it was her. They've picked him up and he's at headquarters now. I've got some photos of the girl with me. I'm hoping he will identify her.'

'Is the other guy badly hurt?'

'He's taken a nasty bang on the head, but he's all right. Who hit him? If this girl was Odette Malroux, what was she doing in a joint like the Prates' Cabin?'

'Maybe it wasn't her.'

'We'll soon see.'

Ten minutes later, we were in Sergeant Hammond's office. With him was the barman of the Pirate's Cabin. I recognized him as the man Odette had spoken to.

Renick showed him a selection of photographs of the girl.

'That's her,' the barman said. 'That's her for sure.'

'What time did she come in?' Renick asked, looking significantly at me'

'A little after nine o'clock.' She looked around as if expecting someone, then she asked me if there was another bar. I told her no, and showed her where the restaurant was. She checked the restaurant, then started to leave. There was a guy with a load on: he wasn't boiled, but he had had plenty. He grabbed hold of her arm as she passed him. She shook him off and went out. He followed her.'

'Then what happened?'

'About ten minutes later some guy comes in and says there's a man lying in the car park. I went out and found this drunk. He was bleeding badly so I called a cop.' 'Any cars leave the parking lot before he was found?' 'A few minutes after the girl left I heard two cars start up and leave. One of them was a high powered sports car: I could tell that by the noise it made.'

'And the other one?'

'Just a car.'

'So the girl came into the bar as if expecting to meet someone and then she left?'

'That's correct.'

'How was the girl dressed?'

The bar man gave a pretty good description of the clothes Odette had worn that night and Sergeant Hammond jotted down the description.

When the barman had gone, Renick said, 'I guess we'll call on this guy in hospital. What's his name, Sergeant?'

'Walter Kerby.'

We found Walter Kerby lying in bed, his head in bandages and looking pretty sorry for himself. He admitted right away that he had been drunk on Saturday night.

'I saw this dish,' he said, 'and I thought she was a push over. No decent girl goes to that joint. She turned snooty, but I thought it was the old come-on so I went out into the parking lot after her. I guess I was wrong about her. I was fooling around with her and she didn't like it. Then all of a sudden, some guy comes out of the darkness and clubs me over the head. That's all I know about it.'

'What was he like?' Renick asked.

I was standing on the other side of the bed and I was scared Kerby would hear my heart beats.

'He was a big guy. I wouldn't recognize him again. I never did see his face. It was dark, and he was fast. I didn't stand a chance.'

On the way back to the office, Renick said, 'Why did she go to the Pirates' Cabin? She had a date with her girl friend to go to the movies. They were to meet at nine o'clock ' but just after nine she arrives at this joint. What made her change her mind?'

'Could be she had a telephone call.'

'Yeah. That could be the answer. Was she kidnapped at this joint?– I'm going to get a check on Kerby. He could have

82

been connected with the kidnapping although I don't think so. I'll get O'Reilly to see if he can find out if she did have a telephone call before she left home.'

It wasn't until five o'clock that Renick got the information he wanted. He came into my office and sat on my desk.

'At a quarter to nine, just before the girl was leaving for the movies, she did get a call,' he told me. 'It was from a friend of hers: Jerry Williams. I've checked on Williams. He's a student at the College of Medicine. The girl and he go, out together occasionally. He mixes in her set. We've got nothing against him. I've talked to Meadows. He's against questioning Williams. I guess we'll just have to wait for something to happen.'

'Want me to stick around?'

Renich shook his head.

'If I want you in a hurry, I can always reach you at your home.

'I have a date tonight,' I said. 'I could be late.'

'That's okay, Harry. You keep your date. If I want you, I'll send a call out for you. Where will you be?'

I had anticipated this, and I was ready for him.

'At the Casino restaurant. I'll be leaving there about one. You can get me at home after two.'

After he had gone, I telephoned Nina.

'I'm going to be late I told her. 'This thing I told you about is developing. I shall be moving around. I told John if he wants me after two, I'll be home.'

Then leaving the office, I drove down to the beach cabin to wait.

CHAPTER SEVEN

I

AT twelve-thirty, I left the cabin and drove to the bus terminus. I parked the Packard and walked over to the Inquiry desk. I asked the girl if the eleven o'clock plane from Los Angeles was on schedule. She said it was, and the bus from the airport would arrive at one-five.

I then shut myself in a phone booth and called police headquarters. Sergeant Hammond told me that Renick had just gone home. There was nothing new on the Malroux case.

It was now time to call Malroux.

In the letter I had drafted for Odette to her father, he had been told to stand by for a telephone call after midnight when he would be given last-minute instructions for delivering the ransom.

He was standing by all right. He answered my call himself.

'You know who this is,' I said, making my voice hard and tough. 'Have you got the money?'

'Yes.'

'Okay: here's what you do,' I said. 'Leave your house at two o'clock. You'll be watched. Come in your Rolls. Drive along East Beach Road Somewhere along the road you'll see a flashing light. Don't stop. As you pass the light, drop the bag out of the car window and keep going. Go to Lone Bay parking lot. You'll find your daughter's car there. If the money is okay, and you haven't tried to pull a fast one, your daughter will join you. It'll take about an hour to get her to you. Expect her around three. If she doesn't turn up at three, go home, you find her there. Have you got all that?'

'I understand.'

'That's it then. No tricks. Come alone. From the moment you leave the house, you'll be watched. You don't have to worry about the girl. She's fine, but she won't be if you pull a fast one.'

'I understand!'

I had to hand it to him. He sounded unmoved and very, very calm.

I hung up, then leaving the terminus, I crossed to the Packard, got in and lit a cigarette.

I wasn't unmoved nor was I very, very calm. If it hadn't been for the thought of those two tapes in the bank that must give me protection against a prosecution if anything turned sour, I wouldn't have gone through with thing. With the tapes, to safeguard me, and the thought that by tomorrow I would be worth fifty thousand dollars, I managed to screw up my nerves to finish the job.

I kept assuring myself that nothing could go wrong. So far, Rhea had been justified in predicting her husband's reactions. It seemed to me, and I was groping for comfort, that the chances of him calling in the police when Odette returned was now remote.

The police would of course, question Odette about the bashed wing of her car, and this I had warned her about. But with a man of Malroux's influence behind her, the police couldn't become too curious nor could they push her around.

I looked across at the bus terminal. There were a few people waiting for the bus. There were only about five other cars, besides mine, in the park. No one paid any attention to me. I was just another man, waiting for someone off the bus.

A few minutes after one o'clock I saw the headlights of the bus as it came down the road. It swung to a standstill outside the terminus. There were about two dozen people in the bus. I leaned forward to stare anxiously through the wind-shield for the sight of Odette.

After a moment or so I spotted her. She was wearing the sun goggles, the red wig and the cheap blue and white dress. As she moved away from the bus, she looked anxiously around. She seemed pretty nervous.

I slid out of the Packard and went over to her.

There was a crowd of people milling around: some of them waiting for taxis: some greeting friends.

Odette saw me coming and started towards me. We met by the bus.

'Hello there,' I said. 'The car...'

A heavy hand dropped on my shoulder: a hand that could belong to a cop. For a moment I was completely paralysed. Then I looked around, my heart skipping every other beat.

A broad-shouldered, suntanned man of around fifty stood grinning at me.

'Harry! Well, what do you know! How's the ex-jailbird!'

I recognized him immediately. His name was Tim Cowley. He was a reporter for the *Pacific Herald:* a first rate newspaper man who visited Palm City fairly regularly, and with whom I had worked and played golf whenever he came my way.

The unexpected sight of him threw me in such a panic I couldn't utter a word.

I grabbed hold of his hand and shook it, slapping him on the shoulder while I made a frantic effort to gain control of myself.

Odette just stood there. I wanted to scream at her to go away.

'Why... Tim!'

Somehow I managed to get my voice going.

'I've just blown in. How are you, boy?'

'I'm fine. Good to see you again...'

The shrewd, ever-curious eyes moved from me to Odette.

'Hey ... don't keep a lovely like this to yourself. Introduce me, you dope.'

'This is Ann Harcourt,' I said. 'Ann, this is Tim Cowley: a great newspaper man.'

Too late, Odette seemed to realize the danger. She backed away, looked at me and then at Cowley and seemed on the point of bolting. I reached out and caught hold of her wrist.

'Ann's a friend of Nina's,' I said to Cowley, 'She's passing through to Los Angeles and she staying the night with us.' My fingers dug into her wrist. 'What are you doing here, Tim?'

With his eyes still on Odette, 'The usual grind. Have you a car here, Harry? Can you drop me off at the Plaza?'

'I'm sorry... I'm going the other way. Nina's waiting for us.' I looked at Odette. 'The car's over in the park. Wait for me, will you?' I gave her a shove, sending her on her way across the road towards the car park.

I saw Cowley looking after her, one eyebrow lifted.

'That kid is so shy,' I said, 'she just freezes at the sight of any man.'

'That's a fact. She looked scared to death. What's biting her?'

'She's just a sex-conscious kid. She and Nina get along fine, but she drives me nuts.'

It was the right thing to say for he suddenly grinned.

'I know kids of her age get like that. What are you doing now, Harry?'

I told him I was working for the District Attorney.

'We'll get together and have a talk,' I said. 'I mustn't keep this kid waiting or she'll lay an egg.'

'Okay. I'm at the Plaza. See you, Harry'

I left him and crossed to the Packard. As I got in, I said, 'What's the matter with you? Why did you stand there like a dummy?'

She looked resentfully at me.

'He had seen you speak to me. I thought it was better to stay.'

'Well, at least he couldn't recognize you. I'm sure of that. It was bad luck. . .'

'What's all this about the police? I've been going crazy after that telephone call of yours. How have the police come into it? Has father.. .?'

'No and I don't think he will call them in. It was another bit of bad luck.'

I told her the whole story. When I was through, I said, 'You'll have to have an explanation for the bust wing. You can say you did it when you came out of the garage. I don't know how far Renick will press you. He might ask where you have been. If he does, tell him to mind his own business. This hit and run story is phoney. I don't think he will press you, but you have to be ready for him.'

'You seem to have handled this pretty badly,' she said.

'Why didn't you tell me about the accident?'

'Oh, forget it!' I was getting fed up with criticism. 'Nothing happened your end? You stayed in the hotel and kept off the streets?'

'Yes.'

'You haven't forgotten all the dope I gave, you, just in case your father calls in the police.'

'I haven't forgotten.'

It was twenty minutes to two when we reached the cabin. I pulled up and gave her the key.

'Go in there and change and wait for me. I should be back around two-thirty.'

She took the key and got out of the car. I handed her the suitcase.

'I'll be waiting,' she said. She suddenly smiled at me. .'Take care of that money, Harry.'

'I'll take care of it.'

87

She leaned into the car.

'Kiss me.'

I put my arm around her shoulders and pulled her to me. Our lips touched. She drew away, her finger touching her mouth.

'It's a bore you're married, Harry.'

'That's the way it is,' I said, staring at her. 'But don't kid yourself . . . I wouldn't swop.'

'That's what I mean... it's a bore.' I started the car.

'I'll be seeing you.'

She stood back and as I drove down East Beach Road, I saw her in my driving mirror, walking slowly back to the cabin.

I had already chosen the spot from where I would signal Malroux. There was a big thicket behind which I could hide the car. There was also plenty of cover for me, and I had a clear, uninterrupted view of the road.

I drove the car off the road, turned off the lights, walked back to the road to satisfy myself the car couldn't be seen. I then squatted down behind a bush, my flashlight in my hand and waited.

It wouldn't take Malroux more than ten minutes to reach this spot if he left his house punctually at two. I had just time for a cigarette.

As I squatted there, smoking, my nerves seemed to be crawling out of my skin. Suppose Malroux was planning a trap?

Suppose he had brought O'Reilly along with him and when they saw my light, O'Reilly, a tough ex-cop, jumped out of the car and went for me?

I tried to assure myself Malroux wouldn't, risk his daughter's life, but suppose he had guessed this was a faked kidnapping? Suppose...?

Then I saw distant headlights and I hurriedly stubbed out my cigarette.

This was it, I thought, in another few seconds I'd know if I had walked into a trap.

In the moonlight, I could see the car. It was the Rolls. I let it come closer, then pushing my torch through the shrub, I began pressing the button on and off, sending a flicking beam into the road.

The Rolls was moving at about twenty miles an hour. I could see there was only the driver in sight. But that didn't mean anything. If O'Reilly was with him, he would be hidden at the back.

The car was level now. It slowed slightly. I saw Malroux make a movement, then with an effort, he tossed a bulky briefcase out of the window. It landed with a thud in the road within ten feet of me.

The Rolls gathered speed and swept on, heading for Lone Bay.

I remained squatting behind the bush, staring at the briefcase lying on the road for several seconds, scarcely believing the money was there, and within my grasp.

I looked down the road. The red tail lights of the Rolls were fast disappearing in the distance. I stood up, grabbed the briefcase and·ran back to the Packard. I threw the briefcase on the back seat, slid under the driving wheel and drove fast towards the beach cabin.

I was elated. It had turned out to be the easiest job in the world, and now I was worth fifty thousand dollars!

I reached the cabin as the hands of the clock on the car's dashboard showed twenty-five minutes to three. I parked the car and got out, reaching into the back for the briefcase. Then I paused to look around. There was no other car in the park, and that surprised me.

Rhea should have been here by now. They couldn't have walked. Then where was her car?

Maybe, I told myself, she had had trouble getting away. Maybe O'Reilly had been on the alert, and she would be late. That wasn't my funeral. I wasn't going to wait for her. I would take my cut, give the rest to Odette and get home.

I hurried across the sand to the cabin which was in darkness. That wasn't unexpected. Odette would be sitting on the veranda waiting for me. She wouldn't have put on the lights in case someone, passing, might wonder what was in the cabin at this late hour.

But when I walked up the veranda steps there was no sign of her. I paused, suddenly uneasy.

'Odette!'

No sound came to me. The air conditioner was on. Cold air came out of the cabin and dried the sweat on my face.

I entered the cabin, shut the door, put the briefcase on the table and groped for the light switch. I turned on the light.

The room was just as I had left it a few hours ago.

I listened, puzzled and very uneasy.

'Odette!' I raised my voice. 'Hey! Are you there?'

The silence in the cabin was now frightening me. Had she lost her nerve and bolted? Or maybe she had fallen asleep while waiting for me'

I crossed the room and opened the bedroom door. My hand ran down the wall until my fingers found the light switch. I flicked it on.

Just for a brief moment I relaxed when I saw her lying on the bed. Her face was turned away from me. Her black hair was spread out on the pillow. The red wig lay on the floor at the foot of the bed.

'Hey! Wake up! I've got the money!' I said, then a cold chill began to crawl up my spine.

Twisted tightly around her throat, cutting into her flesh, was something that looked like a nylon stocking.

I took two, slow hesitant steps forward and I peered at her. I caught a glimpse, of the blue skin, the protruding tongue and the flecks of white foam around her lips. Shuddering, I stepped hurriedly back.

I just stood there, my heart scarcely beating, while I tried to accept the fact that she had been brutally and horribly strangled.

II

This was murder!

With my mind paralysed with shock, I walked unsteadily into the lounge and across to the bar. I poured myself a shot of Scotch. It helped steady me.

Where was Rhea? I looked at my watch. It was now three minutes to three. Why hadn't she come? I had to know if she was coming.

After hesitating for some moments, I reached for the telephone and called her house.

I recognized the butler's voice as he said, 'Mr. Malroux's residence. Who is this, please?'

He didn't sound as if he had been dragged out of bed. Probably, he was sitting up, waiting for Malroux to return.

'Mrs. Malroux,' I said. 'She is expecting me to call. Tell her it is Mr. Hammond calling.'

'I am sorry, sir, but Mrs. Malroux is asleep. I can't disturb her.'

'I must talk to her. She's expecting me.'

'I'm very sorry, sir.' He almost sounded sorry. Mrs. Malroux isn't well. The doctor has given her a sedative. She is not to be disturbed.'

'I didn't know. Well, thanks,' and I hung up.

What did this mean? I asked myself. Was her illness an excuse so she could slip out of the house and not be missed or had she become really ill?

I wiped my sweating hands.

By now Malroux would be at the Lone Bay parking lot, and waiting. When Odette didn't show up, he would return home. How soon would it be before he alerted the police?

Then a sudden horrible thought dropped into my mind that set my heart pounding. Those two tapes, so safely lodged in the bank, were useless to protect me now. A faked kidnapping was one thing, but murder was something else. This murder could be pinned on me. The police would say Odette and I had quarrelled over dividing the money, and I had killed her.

I couldn't leave her body here. I would have to get rid of it. If I left it here, Bill Holden would find it and call the police. They would want to know who had rented the ,cabin and he would name me. They would want to know why I had rented this de luxe cabin for close on two weeks when I had been out of a job and had no money. They would want to know where I had been this night. Tim Cowley had seen me with a girl. I had introduced her to him as Ann Harcourt. The police would check, and when they found Ann Harcourt didn't exist, they could easily put two and two together and make her Odette Malroux.

How would Rhea react when she learned that Odette had been murdered? Would she admit planning a faked kidnapping and accuse me of killing Odette? I had to talk to her!

But first I had to get rid of Odette's body.

The thought of touching her made me feel sick, but I had to do it. I would have to dump her somewhere where she wouldn't be found until I had had a chance to talk to Rhea.

I decided to take the body to an old worked out silver mine, a mile off the highway. It had the advantage of being on the road home and was a very unfrequented spot. Out there, she could remain undiscovered for months— maybe no one would ever find her.

I hated to do such a brutal thing to her, but I had to think of myself. I took another drink, then bracing myself, I went out and moved the Packard closer to the cabin. I unlocked the trunk of the car and opened it. Then I returned to the cabin and went into the bedroom.

Without looking at her, I flicked the bed cover over her and picked her up. She was surprisingly heavy, I carried her out to the car and slid her into the trunk, then as gently as I could, I pulled the bed cover from under her and then closed the trunk.

By then I was feeling pretty bad. I went back to the cabin and took another drink, then I went into the bedroom, straightened the bed and put the cover on. I put the red wig in her suitcase and checked to make sure there was nothing else belonging to her I had overlooked. Satisfied, I went into the lounge.

As I was crossing to the door, I saw the briefcase on the table. I had completely forgotten about the money. I was no longer interested in it anyway. I didn't dare touch it. It was murder money. It would have to be dumped with Odette's body.

I grabbed up the briefcase, then turned off the light and locking the cabin, I got in the car.

I had a three mile drive. Before reaching the mine, I had to pass through Palm Bay. The mine was between Palm Bay and Palm City. The time was now ten minutes after three. There would be no traffic, but there would be patrolling cops. I would have to be careful: no fast driving. I mustn't do anything that would attract attention to myself.

I drove on to the highway.

It was as I was driving down the main street of Palm Bay that my plan to get rid of Odette's body blew up in my face.

At the intersection, I spotted a cop, standing by the traffic lights. The lights flickered to red when I was within forty yards of them. I eased down on the brake bringing the Packard to a smooth standstill.

I sat motionless, trying to behave as if I didn't exist, aware the cop was idly staring at me because he had nothing else to stare at.

It seemed to me, he and I were the only two people left on earth. The gay neon lights of Palm Bay flashed on and off, entirely for our benefit. The heavy, yellow moon floated in a cloudless sky and shone down on us. There was no sign of any other person in the broad, long, long road.

I stared at the red light, willing it to change to green. It seemed symbolic to me: it screamed danger to me, and I gripped the steering wheel so tightly my fingers ached.

The cop cleared his throat, then spat in the road. The sound made me start and I looked quickly at him.

He was swinging his night-stick aimlessly, and he was staring at me. He was a big, solidly built man with a round ball-like head that seemed to sit on his vast shoulders as if he had no neck.

Would the lights never change?

I felt sweat on my face and I shifted my eyes back to the glaring red warning sign just ahead of me.

Then it flicked to green.

I took my foot off the brake and with infinite care, I pressed down on the gas pedal, meaning to move smoothly away, doing nothing to incite the cop's criticism.

The car moved forward, then there was a sudden jarring sound and the car jerked sharply to a standstill.

I shifted the gear from 'drive' to 'neutral', and then back to 'drive'. I pressed down on the gas pedal. The engine roared, but the car didn't move.

I sat there, with panic crawling over me, knowing that at long, long last, and after years of good service, the gearbox had finally packed up. Some cog had lost its final tooth, and now I was stuck with a cop within ten feet and me and Odette's dead body in the trunk behind me.

I couldn't move nor think. I just sat there, gripping the driving wheel, not knowing what to do.

93

The green light flicked to red again.

The cop took off his cap and scratched his shaven head. The light of the moon played on his red, brutal face. He was of the old school: a man of about fifty. He had seen everything bad, everything rotten and he had been, and still was, hated by those he also hated. He was a man who would rather get you into trouble than out of it.

I slid the gear lever into reverse, hoping I could move the car from the middle of the road to the kerb, but the reverse gear didn't respond.

The red light flicked to green again.

The cop stepped off the sidewalk and came over.

'Planning to sleep here the night, buster?' he said in a hard cop voice that went with his face.

'Looks like I've got a bust gearbox,' I said.

'Yeah? What are going to do about it?'

"Is there a garage open anywhere close?'

'I'm asking the questions, buster. I'm asking you what you are going to do about it?'

'Get a tow,' I said, trying to keep my voice under control.

'Yeah? And what's going to happen to this heap while you're fixing a tow?'

'Maybe you'd give me a hand and we could push it to the kerb.'

He rubbed his night-stick against his thick, red ear and he squinted at me.

'Yeah?' He spat into the road. 'Do I look the kind of mug who pushes cars belonging to unlucky punks? I'll tell you something: I hate cars and I hate punks who own cars. Get this goddam heap off the middle of the road or I'll book you for obstruction.'

I got out of the car and tried to push it, but it was standing on a slight gradient and I couldn't move it. I pushed until the sweat rolled off of me and the cop watched, his ball-like head cocked on one side, watching.

'You need some iron in your bones, buster,' he said, and slouched forward. 'Okay: relax You can consider yourself booked. Let's have a look at your licence.'

The effort of trying to move the car had left me breathless.

94

I handed him my licence and I had enough sense to give him also my brand new Press card. He stared at the Press card, then at me, then back to the Press card.

'What's this?' he asked.

'I work for District Attorney Meadows,' I said. 'I'm Lieutenant Renick's man.'

'Renick?' The cop pushed his cap to the back of his head. 'Why didn't you say so before? The Lieutenant and me were buddies before he got promoted.' He fingered the Press card doubtfully, then gave it back to me. 'Well, I guess it won't kill me – I'll give you a hand.'

Together we shoved the car to the kerb.

The cop surveyed the car, and expression of disgust on his face.

'A bust gearbox, huh? That's going to cost you plenty to put right, isn't it?'

'I guess so.' My mind was racing. What was I going to do? I didn't dare leave the car in a garage. The only possible thing was to get the car to my garage. But then what was I going to do with Odette's body?

'Well, I guess you guys who own cars must expect to spend dough. Me – I wouldn't own a car if someone gave me one,' the cop went on.

'Is there a garage anywhere around?' I asked, wiping my sweating face with a handkerchief.

'About a mile up the road, but it'll be shut. If a squad car passed and spots this heap, they'll have it towed to headquarters, and then you'll get booked.'

Across the way I saw an all-night drug store.

'I guess I'll phone,' I said.

'Best thing. I'll stick around. Tell the guy I want him to move the heap. I'm O'Flagherty. He knows me.' He took out his guide book and gave me the telephone number of the garage.

I went over to the drug store and phoned the garage. There was a long delay before a man's voice, sleepy and surly, came on the line. He demanded what the hell I wanted.

I told him I wanted a tow and that Officer O'Flagherty had given me the garage number.

The man cursed fluently, but finally he said he would come.

I went to the Packard.

'He's coming,' I said.

The cop grinned.

'I bet he cursed.'

'He certainly did.'

'When you see the Lieutenant, tell him, I think of him,' O'Flagherty went on. 'He's a fine man. He's the best man we have had on the force.'

'I'll tell him.'

'Well, I guess I'll be on my way. See you some time.'

'I hope so, and thanks.'

His red, hard face split into a grin.

'We guys have got to stick together,' and nodding, he started off down the road, swinging his night-stick and whistling under his breath.

I lit a cigarette and with a shaky hand. I was in such a panic was I could scarcely breathe. When I got the car into my garage, what was I going to do? There was Nina to think of. How was I going to move Odette's body without being certain Nina wouldn't suddenly walk into the garage just when I was doing it? I couldn't do it in daylight. Nina never went out at night. I was in such a jam, I couldn't think straight. My mind was seething with panic.

After a ten-minute wait, the breakdown truck arrived. The garage man was a little guy, thin as a bean stick and Irish to his backbone. He was in such a rage, he didn't speak to me but got in the Packard, tested the gears, got out and spat in the street.

'Busted gearbox,' he said. 'A two-week job, and it'll cost plenty.'

'I want you to tow me home,' I said.

He stared at me.

'Don't you want me to repair the goddam thing?'

'No. I want you to tow me home.'

His face worked convulsively.

'You mean you got me out of bed at this hour and I don't get the repair job?'

I had had enough of Irishmen for one night.

'I work for the District Attorney,' I said. 'Stop yakkiting and tow me home.'

I thought he was going to burst a blood vessel, but somehow he managed to swallow his anger. Muttering under his breath, he fixed the tow cable. I told him where to go, and I got in beside him in the truck.

Neither of us said a word during the four-mile drive home. As we pulled up outside the bungalow, I looked anxiously at the windows, but no lights showed. Nina was in bed and asleep.

He cast off the tow line.

'We'll shove her into the garage,' I said.

He didn't help much, but the approach to the garage was on a gentle incline, and after a slight struggle, we got the car in.

'How much?' I asked.

Scowling at me, he said, 'Fifteen bucks.'

I hadn't got fifteen bucks. I took out my wallet. The most I could scrape together was eleven dollars. I gave him ten.

'That's plenty for a job like this.'

He took the bills, glared at me, then got in the truck and drove off.

I closed the garage doors and locked them.

Already the faint light of dawn was showing in the sky. In another hour the sun would come up. There was nothing I could do now. I still had no idea what I was going to do.

In the meantime, all during the day, the body would have to remain in the trunk. The thought turned me sick.

I walked up the path, unlocked the front door and entered the lounge. I caught sight of myself in the wall mirror. I looked like a man in a nightmare.

On the table was Nina's handbag. I opened it and took from it the duplicate set of keys of the car and dropped them into my pocket. I didn't dare risk her opening the trunk while I was at the office.

I turned off the light and went silently into my dressing-room and stripped off my clothes. I took a shower. My mind was still too paralysed with fear for me to begin to think what my next move was to be.

I was reaching for my pyjamas when I heard the telephone

bell ring. The sound made my heart contract. I pulled on my pyjama trousers and bolted into the lounge and snatched up the receiver.

'Is that you, Harry?' I recognized Renick's voice. 'Malroux has just phoned. She has been kidnapped! Come on down to the headquarters right away.

I stood there, shaking, gripping the telephone, feeling wave after wave of panic run through me.

'You hear me, Harry?'

I got control of myself.

'Yes, I hear you. My goddam car has broken down. I've got a bust gearbox.'

'Okay. I'll send a squad car. It'll be with you in ten minutes,' and he hung up.

'Harry ... what is it?'

Nina was standing in the doorway, half asleep.

'It's an emergency. That girl has been kidnapped,' I said, moving past her. 'You go back to bed. They are picking me up right away.'

I was dressing hurriedly as I spoke.

'Can I get you some coffee?'

'Not a thing. Go back to bed.'

'Well, if you're sure...'

'Go back to bed.'

I was struggling into my coat when I heard a car pull up.

'Here they are now.'

I put my arm around her, kissed her, then I ran out to the waiting police car.

CHAPTER EIGHT

I

RENICK was waiting for me in the Operations Room at police headquarters. He, Barty, the Federal Agent, and Captain of Police Reiger were studying a large wall map of the district as I came in.

Renick moved away from the map and joined me.

'Well, here we go. Malroux paid the ransom and, of course, his daughter hasn't been returned. We're going over to talk to him now. I want you along, Harry.'

'What happened then?'

'The kidnappers told him his daughter would be at the Lone Bay parking lot. She didn't show, so he called us.' He turned to. Reiger. 'Captain, can you collect her car and get it photographed? I'll need prints when I get back.' To me, he went on, You'll have to get the picture of the car in every newspaper: we want a complete local coverage.

Reiger said, 'I'll fix it, and I'll get the road blocks organized. In an hour, this district will be sewn up so tight a fly won't get-out of it.'

'Let's go, Fred,' Renick said to Barty, and taking my arm, he strode off down the passage, down the stairs to the waiting police car.

As we were being rushed to Malroux's place, Barty, a thick-set man in his early forties, said, 'She's dead of course. If only the old fool had alerted us to we could have marked the money.'

'I can't say I blame him,' Renick said. 'In his place, I would have done the same. Money means nothing to him. He wants his daughter back.'

'He should have guessed they wouldn't return her. You know, John, the more I think about this, the more certain I am it's a local job.'

'That's what I think.'

I stiffened to attention.

'How do you figure that out?' I asked.

'Before she left for the movies,' Renick said, 'she got a telephone call from this guy Jerry Williams. As soon as Malroux alerted us, I telephoned Williams, but he wasn't there. He's in hospital with a bust leg and he's been there since Thursday so he couldn't have telephoned the girl. That means it was the kidnapper using Williams's name. How did he know about Williams? The boy's father tells me the boy hasn't seen Odette for a couple of months. Think that one over. Then another thing: why pick on the Pirates' Cabin. Okay it's an out of the way

99

place, but there are plenty of other lonely places better known than that joint. It's very unlikely a stranger to the town would know of it.'

While he was speaking the police car pulled up outside Malroux's house. The lights were on on the ground floor, and the front door stood open. I could see the butler waiting for us at the top of the steps.

He took us immediately to Malroux who was sitting in a vast room, lined with books and crowded with heavy antique furniture.

Malroux looked haggard and ill.

'Come in, gentlemen,' he said, 'and sit down. I suppose you are going to tell me my daughter is dead.'

'We won't say that yet, sir,' Renick said awkwardly. 'There's still hope she'll turn up. You knew she had been kidnapped when I called on you this morning?'

'Oh yes. This man threatened to kill her if I called you in. It was a difficult decision to make, but I finally decided not to tell you.'

'I understand that. When did you last see your daughter?'

'On Saturday night. She was going to the movies with a friend. She left about nine o'clock. Her friend telephoned about twenty minutes to ten to say Odette hadn't arrived. This didn't worry me. Odette is always changing her mind. She had a telephone call from young Jerry. Williams just as she was leaving the house. I thought she had joined him. A little after half past eleven, the kidnapper telephoned.. He demanded a ransom of five hundred thousand. He warned me not to call in the police. He told me to have the money ready by today and I would receive instructions how to deliver it to him. I had a letter from Odette on Monday morning. I have it here.'

He produced the letter I had drafted and handed it to Renick who read it.

'This is your daughter's handwriting?'

'Yes.'

Malroux then went on to tell Renick about the instructions I had given him, how he had driven along East .Beach Road, had seen the flashing light, had dropped the money from the car and then had driven on to Lone Bay parking lot.

'I found my, daughter's car there. One of the wings had been badly damaged as if she had had an accident. I waited there until three-forty-five, then I realized she wasn't coming. I reported to a policeman who alerted you.'

'He's at the car park now,' Renick said. 'If she should turn up, we'll know at once. You didn't see the man who used the flashlight?'

'No' He was hiding behind a clump of bushes. I only saw the light.'

'We'll want to check those bushes. Would you come with us and show us exactly where?'

Malroux lifted his shoulders wearily.

'I'm a sick man, Lieutenant. The early morning air doesn't agree with me. I anticipated you would want to see the place and I have sketched a map for you.' He passed a slip of paper to Renick who examined it, then passed it to Barty.

'Suppose you go out there and check, Fred?' Renick said. 'As soon as the news breaks, we'll have people trampling all over that spot.' He looked at me. 'You go with him and send the car back for me.'

Barty nodded, and with me trailing after him, he went down to the police car.

'Tough old guy,' he said as we shot away down the drive. 'Damned if I would be so controlled if I had lost my only daughter.'

It gave me a queer feeling when we pulled up by the clump of shrubs behind which I had hidden not three hours ago.

I now had the opportunity of seeing Barty at work, and I was immediately impressed by his efficiency. By now the sun was coming up. He told the two police officers with us to search around for a place where a car could have been hidden, then he investigated the clump of shrubs, warning me to keep away.

After some twenty minutes, during which time I stood around and sweated, he called me over.

'I guess I've got all there is to be got here,' he said. 'You can see where the guy hid. Here's a heel print in the soft earth that'll make a dandy cast. It may not mean a thing unless we

101

catch him wearing the same pair of shoes. Here's a cigarette butt — a Lucky — but that may not mean anything unless we can prove he always smokes Luckies. If he does, we have a swell talking point for the jury.'

One of the police officers came over and told Barty they had found where the car had been hidden.

We joined the other officer where I had left the Packard.

'We have a good impression of a tyre here, sir,' he said as Barty came up. 'There's a lot of oil too. I guess the car could be in trouble. It fairly leaked oil.'

Barty examined the ground and grunted.

'I've a lot of work to do here, Barber,' he said to me. 'Will you take the car and pick John up? Tell him I'll be here for a couple of hours and to send a car for me.'

'Sure,' I said, and leaving the three men, I walked to the police car.

I drove back to Malroux's house. I just couldn't believe this was happening to me. It was like living in a nightmare. I kept hoping I would wake up and find it had never happened. Every now and then my mind went to the Packard in my garage, and I would come out in a cold sweat.

As I pulled up outside the main gates to Malroux's house, I saw Renick waiting. He was carrying a briefcase: it was the same briefcase that Malroux had dropped from his car. It was unmistakable. The sight of it pretty nearly stampeded me.

Renick tossed the case into the back of the car and got in beside me.

'Barty find anything?' he asked.

I told him what Barty had found. My voice was flat and dead. I knew I had left the briefcase in the trunk of the car, and yet, here it was, right behind me.

'What have you got there?' I asked.

'That's like the briefcase Malroux used to hold the ransom money. He had a pair: they are identical. This is a break for us. We'll get the case photographed. You never know. The kidnapper may have dumped the case. We might trace it and get his fingerprints. Right now, we'll report back to Meadows. If he is ready, we'll alert the Press. All we can hope for now is someone will come forward who saw the girl after she left the Pirates' Cabin.'

You won't get anywhere with that angle, I thought. How thankful I was I had insisted that Odette should change her clothes and wear a red wig.

Meadows was waiting for us when we arrived at his office. After Renick's report, he got up and began to pace up and down his office, chewing his cigar.

Finally, he said, 'Well, now we go into bat. We'll be in time for the lunch editions.' He paused to point a stubby finger at me. 'This is your job, Barber. We want Press co-operation. I don't have to tell you what to do. I want plenty of good publicity. Understand?' He swung around to Renick. 'And watch this, John! No mistakes. We'll be right in the limelight. This kidnapper has to be caughtcheck?'

'Yeah,' Renick said. 'I'll talk to Reiger, then we'll get moving with the Press.'

We both went to Reiger's office. He gave me a batch of photographs of the car.

'Okay, you get busy, Harry,' Renick said. 'I want to talk to the Captain.'

I asked him the question I had been wanting to ask for the past hour.

'When you talked to Malroux, did you see anything of his wife?'

I could see Renick's surprise as he shook his head.

'No. Malroux told me she has collapsed and is in bed.'

Reiger looked up sharply.

'Collapsed? I wouldn't have thought she was the collapsing type.'

Renick made an impatient movement.

'So what? She became hysterical last night while they were waiting for the kidnapper to telephone. The doctor had to be called. He gave her a strong sedative, and she hasn't come out of it yet.'

Dry mouthed, I asked, 'You checked with the doctor, John?'

He frowned at me.

'Anything on your mind, Harry?'

'No. Like the Captain just said: she doesn't strike me from her photos as the collapsing type.'

'Look, don't let's waste time about her,' Renick said.

'Whether she is the collapsing type or not, Malroux says she collapsed. Get busy with those prints.' He handed me the briefcase. 'Get this photographed and circulate the prints too.'

'I'll fix it.'

For the next three hours, I didn't move from the telephone. The moment I replaced the receiver, the bell rang again. By ten o'clock the outer office was packed with newspaper men all clamouring for the story.

At ten-thirty, I took the whole crowd of them to Meadows. He certainly could handle newspaper men. Police Captain Reiger and Federal Officer Barty were there, but they didn't get a look in. Meadows hogged the whole show.

Glad of a little respite, I left them with him and returned to my office. As I sat down at my desk, the telephone bell rang. It was Nina.

'Harry, I've lost my car keys and I want to use the car. Did you take them?'

The car!

During the past hectic hours I had forgotten about the car and what was in the trunk.

'I hadn't time to tell you,' I said. 'You can't use the car. The gearbox has packed up. I had to get a tow home last night.'

'What shall I do? I have a lot of pots to take to the shop. Can't we get it fixed? Shall I get someone from the garage...?'

'No! It means a new gearbox. We just can't afford that. Take a taxi. Look, Nina, I'm right up to my eyes. Forget the car. I'll see you some time tonight,' and I hung up.

I hadn't got over that shock before there was a tap on the door and Tim Cowley walked in.

The sight of him jarred me down to my heels.

'Hello, boy,' he said. 'So you're really in the thick of it.'

'You're missing something,' I said. 'The D.A. is holding a Press meeting right now. All the boys are in there.'

He pursed his lips and made a rude noise.

'That old wind-bag! All he thinks about is getting his ugly mug in the papers.' He came in and folded himself down in one of the armchairs. 'When I write my piece about this kidnapping, it's going to be from a completely different angle from those suckers in with your boss. This, Harry' could be the big story if it is handled right and I'm going to handle it right. Renick is a smart boy. I'll talk to him, but not to his boss. He's no use to me.' He lit a cigarette, his quizzing eyes searching my face. 'They reckon she's dead, don't they?'

'That's their guess. They don't know for sure.'

'How's Malroux taking it? I went there, but the house is surrounded by cops. I couldn't get near him.'

'He seems to be taking it pretty well. You must remember he is a dying man. He hasn't more than a couple of months to live.'

'And how's his glamorous wife taking it?' 'She's collapsed.'

Cowley stared at me.

'She's — what?'

'She's under doctor's orders. She has collapsed. You know what the word collapse means?'

He threw his head back and laughed like a hyena.

'That's rich! I would have betted she would have been dancing the can-can on the roof.'

'What do you mean?'

'Look, these people — the Malroux — are French. Do you know anything about the hereditary laws in France?' 'I can't say I do. What has that to do with it?'

'By law, a child inherits half the parents' estate. That means this girl would have got half Malroux's millions. Even if Malroux wanted to give his wife all his money, he couldn't do it. Half what he owns goes automatically and by law to the girl when he dies, and half what he owns must be a very, very large slice of dough.'

I felt a spooky feeling run through me.

'If these kidnappers have murdered the girl, and it seems likely, and if Malroux dies shortly, and that seems likely too, Rhea Malroux inherits the whole fortune. That's why I'm surprised to hear she has collapsed — probably with joy.'

Here then could be the motive for Odette's death: had this faked kidnapping been a blind to set the stage for murder? Had Rhea picked on me for a catspaw?

Cowley said, 'What's on your mind, Harry? You look as if you have swallowed a bee.'

The intercom buzzed at this moment. I flicked down the switch.

'I want you,' Meadows bawled. 'Come on in.'

'His Master's Voice,' Cowley said, grinning.

I got to my feet.

'See you, Tim,' I said. 'Anything I can do, just let me know.'

Glad to escape from his quizzing eyes, I left the office at a run.

II

By midday, the organized search for Odette Malroux had swung into its stride and it was on a scale that had me scared. Every road out of town was blocked. Army personnel from a nearby camp had been called in to help. More than a thousand men, police and troops, were allotted territory in the needle-in-a-haystack hunt for the missing girl. Three helicopters buzzed over Palm Bay and Palm City with a direct radio link to Meadows' headquarters.

Meadows told the newspaper men who still hung around, waiting hopefully. 'We're playing a hunch that she's in the district. We reckon she's dead, but we could be wrong. If she's dead, then it's my guess her body has been dumped somewhere and we are going to find it. If she's still alive, then she could be hidden somewhere close and we are going to find her. Every house, every apartment and farm will be checked. We have plenty of men. It'll take time, but if she's within fifty miles of this office, sooner or later we'll find her.'

Later, when the newspaper men had gone, Renick came in. He had been down to the hospital to talk again to Walter Kerby in the hope Kerby had remembered now something that would give a clue to the kidnapper.

Meadows looked searchingly at him.

'Anything?'

'No. At least he is sure the man was tall and broad shouldered. It doesn't help much, but it is something. We know we are looking for a tall, broad-shouldered man who smokes Luckies, who owns a pretty wackey car, and weighs around one hundred and eighty pounds.'

'How did you get his weight?' Meadows asked.

'From the heel print. Barty experimented. The impression came right when one of his men weighing one hundred and eighty-five pounds trod down on the soil.'

Meadows looked pleased.

'A little more information like that, and we'll be able to put out a composite picture.'

I listened to all this with a tension that made my muscles ache.

Then the door jerked open and Police Captain Reiger came in. His broad fleshy face was alight with excitement.

'We've gotta break!' he said. 'A guy living out at West Beach has reported an accident. His name is Herbert Carey. He owns a drug store at West Beach. Last night, he and his wife were visiting relatives at Lone Bay. He parked his car at Lone Bay parking lot. As he was leaving the parking lot a T.R.3 came into the lot and Carey collided with it.'

While he was talking I went over to the window and lit a cigarette. I kept my back turned to the room. I knew I had lost colour. I was sure they would see so something wrong if they got a look at my face.

'It was the Malroux girl's car. Carey took the number. He admits the accident was his fault. And listen — a man was driving!' As Reiger talked in his hard cop voice, every word he said stabbed into me. 'This guy must have been one of the kidnappers. Although it was Carey's fault, the guy wouldn't stop. He drove to the end of the lot, parked the car and ran off.'

Meadows demanded, 'Why the hell didn't Carey report the accident right away?'

'He does what his wife tells him. It was his fault, and she wouldn't let him admit it. He only made up his mind this morning to report it.'

Renick said,' I want to talk to him.'

'He's on his way down now. I sent a squad car to pick him up. He'll be here any minute.'

'Did he get a good look at this guy?'

'I think so. The park was dark, but at least he talked to him.'

By now I had control of my nerves. I didn't dare meet Carey. I came away from the window.

107

'I guess I'll get back to my desk. I've a whale of a lot of work to do,' I said and made for the door.

'Hey!' Renick said. 'Stick around. I want you to hear what this guy says.'

Would Carey recognize me? Would he walk into his office, stare at me and then say, 'This is the man!'

I went over to an empty desk and sat down. The next twenty minutes were the worst minutes I have ever lived through.

Reiger, who had been studying the wall map' said suddenly, 'You know that Old silver mine off Highway Seven? Could be a place to dump a body. I'd better check it and he picked up the telephone receiver and began to give orders.

These guys are professionals, I thought. Where was I going to hide Odette's body? With road blocks in operation, with over a thousand men already in action, searching, checking house after house, apartment after apartment, how was I going to get rid of the body?

While we waited, the telephone bell kept ringing. Every five minutes or so we got a report of progress. These guys were really working. Already a quarter of the map had been checked. I saw the search was drawing closer to my street. Would they think to check the garage? Would they think to check the car?

There came a sudden knock on the door and in came Herbert Carey and his wife.

They made an odd looking couple. She towered above him. His bald head glistened with sweat and he was twisting his hat nervously as he followed his wife in. Looking at him, not having seen his face in the darkness of the car park, I looked curiously at him. He was one of those weak nondescript characters who always got imposed upon, and who live in nervous bewilderment, never quite sure if he is doing the right thing at the wrong moment or the wrong thing at the right moment.

The woman was big and blowsy with small, hard eyes and an aggressive chin. She was the boss. Anyone could see that. She sailed in as if she owned the place and selecting Meadows as her target, she went into the attack.

The accident, she declared, was not her husband's fault.

The fact the man had run away proved it. What was the idea of bringing them down here? They had their store to look after. Did Meadows imagine an eighteen-year-old chit of a girl could handle the store while they wasted time with the police, and so on and so on with Meadows trying to stem the flood.

I sat there, frozen with panic while I stared at Carey.

Maybe that was the wrong thing to have done. My concentrated stare attracted his attention and he turned suddenly and looked at me.

I felt my heart contract as I saw him stiffen. He looked away, then looked again at me. Our eyes met. I had a horrible feeling that he recognized me. For a long moment we stared at each other, then he turned away, hunching his shoulders, back into his role of bewilderment.

Meadows was explaining to the woman about the kidnapping and she was quietening down.

'I'm not interested in the accident,' he told her. 'I want a description of this man.' He side-stepped her and went over to Carey. 'You talked to him?'

The little man nodded nervously.

'Yes, sir.'

'Tell me what he was like.'

Carey looked at his wife, then back at Meadows. He dropped his hat, picked it up, flushing.

'Well, he was a big fellow, sir. It was dark. I didn't get .a good look at him.'

'Big and broad?'

'That's right.'

'I wouldn't say that,' Mrs. Carey said. "He was broad all right, but he wasn't tall. He was you,' and she pointed at Meadows.

He scowled at her.

'I'm talking to your husband,' he said. 'I'll talk to you later.'

'My husband never notices anything,' the woman said. 'It's no good asking him. His brother's the same. You can no more rely on anything my husband says than you can rely on anything his brother says. I should know. I've been married to him now for twenty-six years.'

Ignoring her, Meadows said, 'You had the impression, Mr. Carey, this man was tall. How tall?'

109

Carey hesitated, looking apologetically at his wife.

'It's hard to say, sir. The light wasn't good. I certainly got the impression that he was tall.'

Meadows made a movement of exasperation. He pointed to Renick.

'That tall?'

Carey stared at Renick, dropped his hat again and fumblingly picked it up.

'Something like it. Maybe a little taller.' The woman snorted.

'I wish I knew what the matter is with you,' she said. 'The man wasn't any taller than this gentleman here,' and again she pointed to Meadows.

'I was under the impression, my dear, he — he was a big man,' Carey said and he wiped his bald head with his handkerchief.

Meadows swung around to me.

'Stand up, will you?' he said impatiently.

I was the tallest man in the room. Slowly, I stood up. My heart was thumping so violently I was scared they would hear it.

'This gentleman is a giant!' the woman said, 'I, keep telling you the other one was not tall at all.'

Carey was staring at me.

'It seems to me.' he said hesitantly, 'this gentleman is about the same size in build and in height to the man in the car.'

I sat down. Carey still continued to stare at me.

'Okay, tell me what happened. You collided with this guy's car?' Meadows said.

Carey dragged his eyes from me.

'I was in my, car and I backed out. I had forgotten to put on my lights, I backed right into his car. I just didn't see it.'

'You did nothing of the kind! You had backed out and this fellow came along and ran into you,' his wife interrupted. 'It was entirely his fault. Then he got abusive and drove away. When he parked his car, he ran off. If it hadn't been his fault, why did he run away?'

'I don't give a damn who's fault it was,' Meadows snarled. 'All I'm interested in is finding this man. Now, sir,' he went on to Carey, 'did you notice anything else about this fellow? Could you make a guess at his age?'

'From his voice and the way he moved, I'd say he was a man in his early thirties,' Carey said. He looked hopefully at his wife. 'Wouldn't you say that, my dear?'

"How can anyone tell by a voice how old anyone is?' his wife snapped. 'My husband reads detective stories,' she went on to Meadows, 'read, read, read — always with his head in a book. People shouldn't read detective stories — they are unhealthy.'

'You couldn't guess his age?' Meadows asked.

'Perhaps I could, but I'm not going to. I don't believe in misleading the police,' and she glared at her husband.

'Did you get an idea what this man was wearing, Mr. Carey?'

The little man hesitated.

'I wouldn't like to say definitely, but I had the impression it was a sports suit. It could have been brown. As he got out of the car, I did think the jacket had pouch pockets.'

'How can you stand there and tell this gentleman all this nonsense I don't know,' his wife said. 'It was dark: you couldn't have seen the colour of his suit; not with your eyesight anyway.' She turned to Meadows. 'Talk about a vain man. He should wear his spectacles all the time. I'm continually telling him. He shouldn't drive without his spectacles.'

'My eyesight isn't all that bad, Harriet,' Carey said, showing a little spirit. 'I only need my glasses for close work.'

Meadows pointed to a newspaper lying on his desk about six feet away.

'Can you read the headlines from where you are standing, Mr. Carey?'

Carey read the headlines without hesitation. Meadows looked over at Renick and shrugged, then he asked, 'Was this man wearing a hat?'

'No, sir.'

Meadows glanced sarcastically at the woman.

'Would you agree to that?'

'He wasn't wearing a hat but that doesn't mean he didn't have one,' the woman said angrily.

111

'Was he carrying one?'

She hesitated, then said crossly, 'I didn't notice.'

While this was going on, Carey was again looking at me, his expression bewildered.

'Mr. Carey,' Meadows said, 'was this man dark or fair?'

'I couldn't say, sir. The light wasn't good enough.'

"He spoke to you?'

'He yelled at us,' the wife put in. 'He knew he was in the wrong. He...'

'Would you recognize his voice again?' Meadows asked paying no attention to the interruption.

Carey shook his head.

'I don't think I would sir. He said very little.'

'What time did the accident happen.'

'Ten minutes past ten. I particularly looked at my watch.'

'Then this fellow ran off. Where did he go?'

'I think he got into a car that was waiting outside the park. Anyway, after he had run off, I heard a car start up and drive off.'

'You didn't see the car?'

'No, but I did see the glare of its headlights.' 'In which direction was the car going?'

'Towards the airport.'

Meadows stopped prowling around the office and stared at Carey, then he looked over at Renick who was taking notes.

'The airport?'

'Well, the car could have been going to West Beach which is beyond the airport. I didn't mean...'

'The airport!' Meadows exclaimed. 'That's an idea.' He suddenly got excited. 'Goddam it! That is an idea! Have we checked the airport, John?'

Renick shook his head.

'No. We reckoned they wouldn't dare take the girl on a plane. We'll check if you think. . .'

'We'll check everywhere,' Meadows said. 'I want a list of all passengers who travelled from the airport from half past ten to midnight. Fix that, John.'

I was now so tense I could scarcely sit still.

Turning to Carey, Meadows said, 'I guess that's all for now, Mr. Carey. Thanks for your help. If there's anything further

I want to know, I'll get in touch with you.' The wife started for the door.

'Come along, Herbert, we've wasted enough time already.'

Carey moved after her, then he paused to look at me. I didn't dare meet his eyes. I pulled open a drawer in the desk and took out some paper as if I had forgotten his existence.

I heard him say to Meadows, 'Excuse me, sir, but who is that gentleman?'

Here it comes, I thought, and icy fingers squeezed my heart. I looked up.

Carey was pointing at me.

Meadows obviously surprised, said, 'That's Harry Barber, my Press officer.'

The woman caught hold of Carey's arm and jerked him to the door.

'For heaven's sake! Come along! If you haven't anything better to do than to waste these gentlemen's time, I have!'

Reluctantly, still staring at me, Carey allowed himself to be led out of the office.

The door closed behind them.

CHAPTER NINE

I

MEADOWS said, 'What a woman!' He sat down behind his desk. 'What do you think, John? I'd bet on Carey's evidence.'

'Oh, sure,' Renick said. 'Anyway, we have another witness: Kerby also said the guy was tall and broad. Well, we're getting somewhere. We now know the man we want is around six foot, weighs one hundred and eighty pounds, was wearing a dark sports suit with pouch pockets, no hat, smokes Luckies, and owns a beat up car. We're about ready to get a composite photo of this guy.' He suddenly turned to me. 'What do you weigh, Harry?'

'Around one hundred and ninety, I guess,' I said huskily. 'What's my weight to do with it?'

'I've an idea. Carey said you were the same build and

113

height as this guy. We'll take a photograph of you, blank out your face and get the papers to print it. We'll ask if anyone saw a man resembling the photograph near Lone Bay parking lot or the Pirates' Cabin.' He looked over at Meadows. 'What do you think, sir?'

'It's a great idea! Meadows said enthusiastically. 'We'll do even better than that.' He called his secretary. 'Miss Leham, I want you to go out right now and buy a sports suit for Mr. Barber. It's got to be in dark brown, and it has to have pouch pockets: something quiet. I want it as fast as you can get it.'

Miss Leham looked me over, nodded and went out.

'While we're waiting, John, get me that passenger list. I want the names of everyone who travelled from the airport between ten-thirty and midnight.' To me, he said, 'How about writing a nice little article about me — a personal thing, about my hobbies, my home life with my kids, my wife: I don't have to tell you. You'll get the dope from the files. See if you can get it into *Time and Newsweek.*'

Back in my office with the door shut, I sat down limply behind my desk. I felt in a trap. This photograph idea of Renick's could be dangerous. Although I was pretty sure no one had seen me at the Pirates' Cabin, I had had enough experience as a newspaper man to know there was always the chance that someone I hadn't seen had seen me. This also applied to the Lone Bay parking lot. At the airport I had stupidly carried Odette's suitcase into the departure hall. The place had been crowded. Any idle watcher might remember me once the photograph appeared.

But the main thing that haunted my mind was how I was going to get rid of Odette's body. I would have to do it tonight. I couldn't keep her in the trunk any longer than tonight. I would have to hire a car. My feeling of panic grew as I remembered how short of money I was. I would have to go to my regular garage and try to talk the owner into lending me a car without paying the usual deposit. I had exactly two dollars in my wallet and I had no idea how much Nina had. I wouldn't be able to draw any money from my job until the end of the week.

Then when I had the car, I had to transfer Odette's body from my car to the other. How was I going to do it without being sure Nina wouldn't suddenly surprise me? It would have to be done when she had gone to bed. I would have to tell her I would be working late, then when she was asleep I would do the job.'

But while I was doing it, suppose one of the searchers spotted me?

My mind cringed at the thought of the awful risk I would have to face.

I had no time to think further about this for the telephone bell started up its continuous clamour. I had to get the articles on Meadows written. Then, as I was finishing the article, Miss Leham came in with the suit, followed by Renick.

It gave me a hell of a jolt when I saw the suit. It was the replica of the one I owned. I had bought my suit soon after I had left jail to have something new to wear.

When Miss Leham had gone, Renick said, 'Change, will you, Harry. The photographer's waiting. We want to get the photos in the last editions.'

I put on the suit and followed him down to the police photographer. In half an hour we had a dozen prints for distribution.

I had a horrible feeling I was committing suicide as I wrote a description of myself and pasted the description to the backs of the photographs. I took the photographs into Meadows' office and gave them to him.

My face in the photograph had been blocked out, but in spite of that, I was still able to recognize myself.

Meadows studied the photographs, nodded, called in Miss Leham and told her to get them to the local papers.

As she was going out, Renick came in.

'I have the passenger lists for you,' he said. 'They don't help. There were only two planes out between ten-thirty and midnight. One to Japan and the other to San Francisco. The Japan plane I've washed out. The 'Frisco plane had fifteen passengers on board. Fourteen of them were business men and their wives. They do a regular trip and the air hostess knows them all personally. The one odd passenger was a girl, travelling alone.'

'That doesn't help. I'm looking for a girl and a man travelling together. There was just the chance the kidnapper had so terrified the girl she might have travelled with him. Who was the lone girl?'

'She's listed as Arm Harcourt,' Renick said. 'The air hostess particularly noticed her. She was a redhead. She was certainly not Odette Malroux.'

The hard cold knot that had formed in my stomach eased a little. My legs felt suddenly so weak I had to sit down.

Meadows flicked the list into the trash basket.

'Well, it was a try. Maybe we'll have more luck with the photograph.'

The time was now after seven. I hung around, listening to the telephone reports of the search until eight, then I said to Renick, 'Okay for me to go home? If anything breaks, you can telephone me.'

'Why, sure, Harry. You get off.'

I returned to my office and called Nina.

'I could be a little late,' I said. 'What are you doing tonight?'

'Why, nothing. I'll wait for you.'

'Look, why don't you go to the movies? Why sit at home on your own? There's a good movie at the Capital. Why don't you take a look at it?'

'I don't want to go alone, Harry. I'll wait for you.'

If only I could get her out of the bungalow for a few hours!

'It'd please me, Nina, if you'd go. You stay home too much.'

'But darling, I don't want to go out alone even if we could afford it. When will you be back? Shall I keep supper for you?'

I gave up. If I went on pressing her to go out, she would become suspicious.

'I guess I'll be about an hour. Yes keep something for me. I'll be seeing you.'

'Oh, Harry, I still haven't found my car keys.' A spurt of irritation ran through me.

'You can't use the car, so why worry? So long for now,' and I hung up.

For a long moment I sat there, staring sightlessly at the desk clock. Usually Nina went to bed around eleven o'clock. I would

116

have to wait until at least one o'clock before I dare move Odette's body. Now the time to act was drawing closer, the horror of the thing I had to do gave me the shakes. But I had to do it. Where was I going to dump the body? Dare I go out to the old silver mine ? I knew it had already been searched. They weren't likely to search it again. If I could get out there without being spotted, her body might never be found. But could I get out there? Before I had left the Operations Room I had studied the map where Renick was plotting the progress of the searchers. They were moving down the highway, away from the silver mine, towards my place. By one o'clock the highway might be clear except for the odd patrolling car. In my official capacity as Press officer to the D.A., I might be able to bluff my way through if – and it was a big if – my nerve held. Right now my nerve wasn't holding. I was in a terrible state.

Before I could do anything, I had to hire a car. That was the first move.

I left the office and took a bus to my local garage. The time was twenty minutes to nine when I walked in.

Ted Brown, an eighteen-year-old youth, who I knew pretty well was sitting in the little office reading a racing sheet. I was relieved to see there was no sign of Hammond, who owned the garage.

'Hi, Ted,' I said, pushing open the door. 'You look pretty busy.'

The boy grinned sheepishly. He laid down his paper and stood up.

'Hello, Mr. Barber,' he said, 'I was just trying to pick a winner. I sure could do with a little luck. The gees haven't been running good for me the whole week.'

'They never run good for me,' I said. 'Look, Ted, I've had some bad luck too. The Packard has packed up. I've got a bust gearbox.'

The boy's face showed his concern.

'Gee! I'm sorry. That's a pretty high item.'

'Yeah. I want to borrow a car for tonight. Have you anything you can let me have?'

'Why, sure, Mr. Barber. There's the Chevvy over there you can take. Just for tonight?'

117

'That's right. I'll bring her back first thing tomorrow.' I started over to the Chevrolet. 'I've a rush date at Palm Bay.

'I'll get you to fill out the form, Mr. Barber. There'll be thirty bucks for the deposit and the insurance.'

I paused.

'I'm in a rush, Ted. I haven't the money on me. I'll settle tomorrow.'

The boy scratched his head, perplexed.

'I don't reckon Mr. Hammond would like that, Mr. Barber. I couldn't do it on my own responsibility.

I forced a laugh.

'What's biting you, Ted? Why, damn it, I've been dealing here for over ten years. Mr. Hammond would be glad to oblige me.'

Ted's face brightened.

'I guess that's right, Mr. Barber. Maybe you'll just sign the form? Then tomorrow when you bring her back...'

'Sure.'

I followed him into the office and waited impatiently while he searched for the form. He finally found it and spread it on the desk in front of me.

As I took out my pen, a car drove into the garage.

It was Hammond.

If I'd only been five minutes sooner I would have been gone by the time he arrived. Now I had an argument on my hands. I knew it when I saw his expression change at the sight of me.

Somehow I managed to give him a grin as he came into the office.

'Hello, Mr. Hammond,' I said. 'You're keeping late hours.'

' 'Evening,' he said curtly. He looked sharply at Ted. 'What's going on?'

'I'm hiring the Chevvy,' I said. 'My car's got a bust gearbox. I'll get you to pick it up sometime next week. I've a rush date in Palm Bay and I must have a car.'

He relaxed a little.

'That's okay. If you'll fill up the form, Mr. Barber. It'll be thirty bucks for gas, insurance and the deposit.'

I began to fill up the form. My hand was so shaky I didn't recognize my own handwriting.

'I'll settle with you tomorrow when I bring her back,' I said as casually as I could. 'This is an unexpected date. I hadn't time to get to the bank before it closed. I'll settle with you tomorrow.'

I signed the form with a flourish and pushed it over to him. He ignored it.

'Give me Mr. Barber's credit card,' he said to Ted.

Ted produced the card, then went out into the garage.

He seemed embarrassed.

Hammond examined the card, then he looked at me and there was a bleak expression in his eyes.

'Mr. Barber, you owe me a hundred and fifty bucks for repairs, gas and oil,' he said.

'Sure thing: I know. I'll settle that tomorrow too,' I said. 'I'm sorry it's run on for so long.'

'I'll be glad if you would.' There was a pause, then he said. 'I'm sorry Mr. Barber, but until the account is settled, I can't give you any more credit.'

I nearly lost control of myself. With my hands in fists, I said, 'Now look, I want a car urgently. I've dealt with you for ten years. This is no way to treat an old customer. I wouldn't ask you to do me this favour if it wasn't urgent.

'There's the bus, Mr. Barber, if you have to go to Palm Bay. Your account has been running unpaid for close on eighteen months,' Hammond said. 'I've spoken to Mrs. Barber about it a number of times. I always get the same story: "I'll settle tomorrow." I'm sorry, but I'm not giving you any more credit. You can have the Chevvy when you have paid the deposit and settled the account. That's final.'

I felt so bad I wanted to die. I had to have that car I My life depended on it!

'I'm in a situation that is very, very urgent, I said, struggling to keep my voice steady. 'I must have a car tonight. I tell you what I'll do. I'll leave my wife's jewellery with you as a deposit. The stuff is worth a couple of hundred bucks. Then tomorrow, I'll pay the whole account. You may not have heard, but I've a job now. I'm the Press officer to the District Attorney.' I took out my Press card and handed it to him.

He glanced at it and handed it back to me.

'If you're working for the District Attorney, Mr. Barber, you'd better get a police car if it's all that urgent. I don't want your wife's jewellery. I don't do my business that way.'

Then suddenly I remembered that in the trunk of the Packard was the briefcase, containing five hundred thousand dollars! What was I doing, standing here, begging this punk to do me a favour when I could buy up his whole goddam garage if I wanted to? I would use some of that money! It was dangerous, but nothing like so dangerous as leaving Odette's body in my garage.

'If that's the way you feel about it, you can go to hell,' I said and I walked out of the garage.

About a mile from home, there was an all-night service station. I would go there when Nina was in bed and hire a car from them, paying them with the money from the ransom bills.

I started down the long road leading to my bungalow. Halfway, I saw two policemen coming towards me on the opposite side of the road. They paused outside a house of a neighbour of mine, then one of them pushed open the gate and walked up the path. The other policeman moved on and went to the house next door.

The house-to-house search had reached my street!

With fear squeezing my heart, I quickened my steps. As I came within sight of my bungalow. I came to an abrupt standstill.

The garage doors I had locked the previous night now stood open!

For a long moment, I just stood there, fighting the urge to turn and run and keep on running. Had the body been found? Were they waiting, out of sight, to arrest me?

One of the policemen had come out of the house across the way. He stared curiously at me.

I braced myself and started down the road towards my bungalow.

II

As I walked up the path, I saw Nina and two soldiers standing by the Packard. At the sound of my approach, the three of them turned.

'Here's my husband now,' Nina said.

'Hello,' I said to her. 'What's going on?'

The two soldiers were no more than kids. One of them was bulky and fair with a fat, pink face. He looked hot and bored. The other was a little guy, dark with a sharp alert expression. He gave the impression of being hostile and tough. I knew at once he would be the one I'd have to handle.

'Is this your car?' the dark one demanded.

Ignoring him, I said to Nina, 'What's all this about?'

'They are searching for the kidnapped girl,' Nina said. She sounded and looked irritated. 'They want the trunk opened.'

By now I had got my second wind. I was so desperate I forgot to be scared.

'You don't imagine I've got her in there, do you?' I said to the fat kid and I managed a laugh.

He grinned awkwardly.

'I guess not, sir,' he said. 'I keep telling Joe here...'

'Will you open this trunk?' the dark one said. 'I've got orders to search every house and car in this street, and that's what I'm going to do.'

'I've told him I have lost my keys,' Nina said. 'I asked him to wait for you, Harry. He's been waiting some time.'

'I'm sorry,' I said to the dark one, 'but I haven't my keys. I've left them with a locksmith. He's cutting a duplicate set for my wife.'

He stared at me: his sharp eyes suspicious.

'That's too bad,' he said. 'I've got a warrant. If you haven't the key, then I'm going to bust this trunk open.' 'I'll have the key here by tomorrow morning,' I said trying desperately hard to sound casual. 'Come tomorrow morning and I'll be glad to open the trunk for you.'

'Come on, Joe,' the fat soldier urged. 'We've got half the goddam street to check yet, and it's getting late.'

Joe paid no attention to him. I could see he was going to make an issue of this.

'I'm going to bust open this trunk,' he said, and moving away from me, he looked around the garage. He spotted a tyre lever and picked it up.

'Now, wait a minute,' I said and I got in front of the trunk.

121

'You're not damaging my car! Here, take a look at this,' and I gave him my Press card.

He stared at it without touching it.

'So what?' He swung the tyre lever impatiently. 'I don't give a damn who you are. I've got orders to check every car in this street: that's what I'm going to do!' I looked at Nina.

'There's a policeman over the way. Go and get him.'

As Nina ran out of the garage, Joe said savagely, 'I don't give a goddam for any cop either. I'm opening that trunk! Get out of my way!'

I remained where I was.

'You're not damaging my car,' I said. 'I'll open the trunk tomorrow morning when I have the key and not before.'

We stared at each other for a long moment, then he put down the tyre lever.

'Okay, if that's the way you want it. Come on, Hank, we're going to shift this punk. I'm opening the trunk!'

'Aw, now look, Joe,' the fat one said uneasily. 'No rough stuff. Let's wait for the cop.'

'I'm obeying orders,' he said. He eyed me. 'Are you getting out of the way or do I have to get you out of the way?'

'You're heading for a court-martial, soldier,' I said.

'You start any rough stuff and you'll be sorry.'

Joe looked at Hank.

'Come on: we're going to shift this guy. If he gets hurt, it's his funeral,' and he started towards me as Nina came up the path with one of the policemen I had seen across the way.

Joe paused as the cop, a big, heavily built man, came into the garage.

'What's going on?' the cop demanded.

'I want to see inside this trunk,' Joe said. 'This guy hasn't the key. I've got orders. I'm busting the trunk open, but this guy says no.'

'Where's the key?' the cop said to me.

'At the locksmith, I told him. 'I'm having a duplicate made.'

He stared at me, scratching his bullet head with a thick finger.

'What locksmith?'

I was ready for that one.

'I don't know. I gave the key to my secretary to fix.' I offered my Press card. 'I work for the District Attorney, officer. I'll have the key here tomorrow morning. I'll willingly open the trunk then. There's nothing in it, but if it will satisfy our friend here, I'll open it tomorrow, but I'm not standing for him busting the lock.'

The cop examined the Press card, then he frowned at Joe.

'Look, soldier, you don't have to bear down on this thing,' he said. 'We know this gentleman. What are you getting so excited about?'

Joe hunched his shoulders. His expression became more hostile.

'I don't give a damn who he is. I've got my orders and I'm going to carry them out.'

'You bust that, lock, soldier,' the cop said, 'and you'll be responsible. You'll have to pay for it.'

'Okay, so I'll pay for it,' Joe said. 'I'm busting it!' The cop shrugged and turned to me.

'Does that suit you Mr. Barber. Let him bust the lock. He'll have to pay for it.'

I was scarcely breathing.

'No, it doesn't suit me,' I said. 'This is an old car. I may not be able to get another lock. This car has a bust gearbox. It's been standing 'in the garage for a couple of days. If you don't believe me, see if you can move it.'

'Yeah?' Joe said. 'So how do we start the motor without the ignition key? Get out of my way! I'm opening this goddam trunk!' and he grabbed up the tyre lever.

I remained where I was.

'Let's settle this,' I said. 'I'll call, Lieutenant Renick. If he wants the trunk opened then okay, this kid can open it.'

The cop's face brightened.

'That's an idea, but I'll talk to the Lieutenant.'

Joe threw down the tym lever in disgust.

'Cops!' His voice was bitter with contempt. 'Okay, hang together, but I'm going to report this to my C.O. Don't imagine you have heard the last of it — you haven't! Come on, Hank, let's get out of here,' and the two soldiers walked down the path, leaving the cop staring uneasily after them.

123

'These kids,' he said in disgust. 'They get a fixed idea, and nothing will shift it.'

'Thanks,' I said, breathing again. 'I was damned if I was going to let him bust my car.'

'You were right. Okay, Mr. Barber.'

He saluted Nina and then went off down the path.

'Well!' Nina said. 'I hated that little beast. I knew he was going to make trouble the moment I saw him.'

I closed the garage doors.

'Better lock it,' I said. 'I don't want him sneaking back here, and he could.'

She gave me the key and I locked the doors.

Together, we went into the bungalow.

'What's been happening, Harry? They think this girl's dead. Everyone is talking about her. What's been happening?' Nina asked as we walked into the lounge.

'I don't know. Get me a drink, will you? I've been at this rat-race all day and I'm about petered out.'

I took off my jacket and tossed it on to the settee, then I sank into a lounging chair and loosened my tie.

Nina mixed a whisky and soda.

'What are we going to do about the car?' she asked. 'It'll have to wait. We can't afford a new gearbox.' She carried the drink over.

'A cigarette?'

'Yes.'

She gave me a cigarette.

'My lighter is in my pocket.'

She went over to my jacket and put her hand in one of the pockets. My mind couldn't have been working. I was so used to having her wait on me.

'Harry!'

The tone of her voice brought me alert.

She was holding my car keys and her car keys in her hand and she was staring at them.

I felt my mouth turn dry.

She looked at me.

'Harry!'

There was a long pause while we stared at each other,

then the glass of whisky I was holding slipped out of my hand and smashed to pieces on the parquet floor.

CHAPTER TEN

I

THE hall clock began to strike nine. The sharp pinging sound of the bell seemed to fill the room.

I got to my feet, staring down at the broken glass and the puddle of whisky on the floor.

'I'll fix it,' I said and started for the door.

'Harry...'

'I'll be right back.'

I had to have a breather. I knew I was chalk white. My mind was seething with panic. I strove desperately to think of a convincing lie, but I couldn't think of one.

I picked up a swob in the kitchen and then started back down the passage to the lounge. I saw Nina fumbling at the front door, trying to open it. When we had come in I had shot the bolts. The top one was stiff and she was trying to draw it back.

'Where are you going?' I shouted to her, throwing aside the swob.

She looked over her shoulder at me. Her face was pinched and white and her eyes unnaturally large.

'To the garage'

She got the bolt back as I jumped forward and grabbed her.

'You're not going out there! Give me those keys!'

'Let go of me!'

She wrenched free and darted away from me, putting her hands behind her back and leaning against the wall. Her breasts under her white shirt rose and fell with her violent breathing.

'Give me those keys!'

'Don't come near me! What have you done?'

'Give me those keys!'

'No!'

I had to have them. I grabbed her, but she twisted away and ran into the lounge. I went after her, caught her wrist and spun her around with her back to me.

'Harry! You're hurting me!

I wrenched open her fingers and got the keys. As we struggled, she slipped and fell on her knees.

I let go of her and stood away, breathing heavily. I felt like hell.

She remained on her knees, her face in her hands and she began to cry.

I dropped the keys into my pocket.

'I'm sorry, Nina.' I could scarcely get the words out. 'I didn't mean to hurt you. Please don't cry.'

I wanted to pick her up but I was too ashamed even to touch her.

She remained on her knees for about two minutes while I stood there, watching her. Then slowly she got up, holding her wrist.

We faced each other.

'You had better tell me the truth,' she said. 'What have you done?'

'I haven't done a thing,' I said. 'Forget it. I'm sorry I hurt you.'

'Will you please give me my car keys? I want to open the trunk of the car.'

'For God's sake, Nina! Will you stop it! I told you to forget it. Don't you understand? You've got to forget it.'

She held out her hand.

'Give me my keys.'

'You little fool!' I said desperately. 'Keep out of this! I'm not giving you the keys!'

She sat down abruptly, staring at me.

'What's in the trunk you're so frightened I'll see — so frightened those two soldiers would see? Harry! Don't tell me that — that girl is in the trunk?'

Sweat was glistening on my face now and I was shaking.

'Listen to me,' I said. 'You've got to pack a bag and go to

126

a hotel! I must be alone here tonight! Will you please, please do what I'm asking and don't ask questions?'

'Oh Harry!' She was staring at me now in horror. 'Tell me it's not true! I can't believe it! Harry! She's not in there, is she?'

'Stop asking questions!' I slammed my clenched fists together. 'Go and pack a bag! Get out of here! Can't you see I have enough on my mind without having to worry about you?'

'Is she dead? She must be dead I Did you kill her?'

I went up to her, grabbed her by her arms and pulling her upright, I shook her.

'Stop, asking questions! You know nothing! Do you understand that? Nothing! Now get out and keep away until tomorrow.'

She pulled free and moved away from me, her hands to her face. Then suddenly she seemed to relax and she lowered her hands.

'I'm not going,' she said, her voice quiet and steady. 'Stop shouting Harry, and sit down. We're going to share this thing. Please tell me what has happened.'

'Do you want me to hit you?' I snarled at her. 'Can't you get it into your head you could go to prison for years if you know anything about this? Don't you understand? I'm trying to save you. You've got to leave here and at once!'

She looked steadily at me, shaking her head.

'The last time you were in trouble you kept me out of it and made me an outsider. You're not doing that to me again. I'm going to help you in any way I can.' 'I don't want your help!' I said violently. 'Now get out!'

'I'm not going, Harry.'

I started a swing, the flat of my hand aiming at her face, but I couldn't hit her. My hand dropped to my side. I stared helplessly at her, feeling completely defeated.

'Did you kill her, Harry?'

'No.'

'But she is in the trunk?'

'Yes.'

"Dead?'

'Yes.'

127

Nina shuddered, and for a long moment the only sound in the bungalow was the steady ticking of the hall clock.

'What are you going to do?' she asked finally.

'I'll hire a car, and take her out to the Petrie silver mine.'

'We haven't the money to hire a car.'

I dropped wearily into the chair.

'I have the ransom money.'

Nina got up and made two drinks. She gave me one and drank the other. Then she sat on the arm of my chair, her hand on mine.

Please tell me. how it happened: right from the beginning.'

'If the police catch up with me,' I said, 'and they find out you know about this, you'll go to jail for ten years; maybe longer.'

'Don't let's think about it.' The touch of her fingers on my hand had a soothing effect. 'Please start right from the beginning. I want to know what happened, and please tell me everything.'

So I told her. I held nothing back. I even told her that Odette and I had been lovers.

'I couldn't leave her in the cabin,' I concluded. 'I was going to hide her in the mine when the damn car broke down.'

Nina's hand closed over mine and gripped it hard.

'You poor darling. You must have had a dreadful time. I had a feeling something was wrong, but I never imagined it could be so terribly bad.'

Somehow, sharing this thing with her, made me feel better. I didn't feel so scared. My mind, up to now frozen with panic, felt more able to cope with what lay ahead.

'Well, now you know,' I said. 'I've no excuse to offer. I did it for the money. It was wrong, but that doesn't help to know that now. If I had waited, this job would have come along, and we could have been happy. I didn't wait and I've got myself into this mess. You must leave me, Nina. I mean it. I can handle it on my own. I don't want you mixed up in it. If anything goes wrong and I'm caught, I couldn't bear the thought of you getting caught too. That would be the last straw. Can't you see that? You must keep out of it.'

She patted my hand, then slid off the arm of my chair and

crossed to the window. She stood with her back to me for several seconds as she looked out into the dark street, then she turned.

'We're going to handle this thing together. Don't let's waste time arguing about it, Harry. When do you think it will be safe to move her?'

'It'll be less risky if I do it around two and three in the morning, but you're not having anything to do with it...'

I'm helping you. Wouldn't you help me if our positions were reversed. Wouldn't I feel you had no real love for me if you let me handle such a thing alone?'

She was right, of course. I shrugged helplessly.

'Yes. All right. Nina, I'm sorry. I was crazy to have done this. I won't argue any more. I'll be grateful for your help.'

She came to me and we held each other. We stood pressed to each other for some minutes, then pushing away from me, she said, 'Is it safe to use that money for the car?'

'It's in small bills. Malroux hadn't time to take the numbers. Yes it's safe to use it.'

'Then you had better arrange about the car now, hadn't you? You can leave it at the top of the road. When you are ready to move her, you can bring it to the garage.'

'Yes.'

I didn't move. I sat there, staring down at the carpet. I would have to open the trunk of the car to get the brief-case. The thought of seeing Odette's body made me quail.

'You'd better have another drink,' Nina said.

She was quick to realize what was going on in my mind.

'No.' I stood up. 'I'm all right. Where's the flashlight?'

She went to a drawer and took out a pocket torch.

'I'll come with you.'

'No. This is something I must do on my own.'

I took the torch, then without looking at her, I went to the front door, opened it and stepped out into the darkness.

The street was very silent. Across the way the windows of a bungalow showed lights. My next door neighbour's house was in darkness. I walked down to the gate and looked up and down the street. There was no one to be seen. My heart was thumping, and there was a sour, sick taste in my mouth.

I walked to the garage doors. I had trouble in fitting the key into the lock. As I opened one of the doors, the faint, but unmistakable smell of death came to me, and I paused, fighting nausea and panic.

I closed the door and turned on my torch. It took me several seconds to screw up my nerve to approach the trunk. It took me nearly a minute to fit the key into the lock.

I stood there, sweat on my face, my breathing hard and fast, my heart pounding while I willed myself to lift the trunk lid.

I swung it up.

The shaking light I held in my hand lit up the cheap blue and white dress, the long, beautiful legs, and the small feet in ballet shoes resting against the spare tyre.

The briefcase lay by the body. I snatched it up and slammed down the lid of the trunk. Sour bile was rising in my mouth and I fought down the urgent need to vomit. My whole body was crawling with the horror of the situation. I controlled myself, forced myself to lock the trunk, then the garage doors and then I walked quickly back to the bungalow.

Nina was waiting. The strain was showing on her face. It seemed to me she was older, thinner and very tense.

I put the briefcase on the table.

'I'll have that drink now,' I said huskily.

She had the drink ready. The whisky braced me. I took out my handkerchief and wiped my face.

'Steady, darling,' Nina said gently.

'I'm all right.'

I lit a cigarette and drew smoke down into my lungs. 'I'll open it,' Nina said and moved to the briefcase. 'No! Don't touch it! Your fingerprints mustn't be found on it.'

I took up the case. There was a clip lock on it: it was easy to open. I pressed down the catch and flicked back the flap over. I turned the case upside down and emptied its contents on the table.

I expected a cascade of money. I expected to see dozens and dozens of packets of currency bills. Instead about thirty newspapers spilled out on to the table: old newspapers, some of them soiled, but just newspapers.

There was no money — just old, soiled newspapers!

II

I heard Nina catch her breath sharply.

I was too stunned to move. I could only stare at the newspapers, scarcely believing what I saw. Then the realization came with the force of a sledge hammer blow.

There was no money — I wouldn't be able to hire a car!

'We're sunk,' I said as I stared helplessly at Nina. 'We really are sunk.'

Nina flicked through the newspapers as if hoping to find some of the money between the folds of the sheets, then she stared at me.

'But what's happened to it? Did someone steal it?'

'No, the briefcase wasn't out of my sight until I locked it in the trunk.'

'But what's happened to the money? Do you think Malroux never intended to pay?'

'I'm sure he intended to pay. The money meant nothing to him. He would have known if he had tried a trick like that he would be risking his daughter's life.' Then I suddenly remembered the other briefcase: the replica Renick had asked me to get photographed.

'There were two briefcases: exactly alike. One of them contained the ransom money, the other these newspapers They must have been switched as Malroux was leaving.

'Who could have switched them?'

'Rhea. Of course! It sticks out like a sore thumb. At the time it struck me as odd that she should have trusted me to collect all that money. I was fool enough to think she had no alternative, but of course she had. She prepared the other case, waited her opportunity and switched the cases. She never had any intention of trusting me or Odette. That's why she didn't come to the cabin. She didn't have to. She had the money before Malroux left the house. I risked my neck for a caseful of newspapers! I'll bet she never even intended to pay me the fifty thousand she promised me. She's played me for a sucker, and she's got away with it!'

Nina said quietly, 'What are we going to do now, Harry?'

That brought me up with a jolt.

'What can we do? Without a car, we're sunk!'

'There are dozens of cars in this street and in Pacific Boulevard that are left out all night. We must take one of those.'

I stared at her.

'You mean — steal it?'

'We borrow it,' Nina said firmly. 'We bring it here, put her in it, then drive it round the corner and leave it. The car will be reported stolen, the police will find it and the girl.' She gripped my hand. 'I can't bear the thought of leaving her in that mine, Harry. She must be found and found quickly.'

I hesitated, but I realized what she had said made sense.

'It's a risk, but you're right. There's no other way.' I looked at my watch. The time was a little after eleven. 'I'll go out and see if I can spot a car that's not locked.'

'I'll come with you.'

'Okay.'

I put the newspapers away in the briefcase, and the case in a cupboard, then we left the bungalow. Arm-in-arm, we strolled up the street like any couple for an airing before going to bed.

We reached Pacific Boulevard that ran parallel with our road. There were a number of cars standing at the kerb on either side of the street. We finally came on an old Mercury, and both of us paused.

'This could do,' I said.

Nina nodded. We looked up and down the street, then she opened her bag and took out a pair of gloves.

'Let me do this,' she said and backed up against the car. As she put on the gloves, she went on, 'Put your arms around me, Harry. Make it look as if we're courting. I'll try the door.'

I took her in my arms.

If anyone was looking out of any of the many windows overlooking the street, they would have seen a man and a woman holding each other, the woman leaning against the car. It was a sight you could see in any street.

Nina said, 'The door isn't locked.'

I drew away from her and looked up at the house before which the car was standing. There were lights on in the upper rooms, but the lower rooms were in darkness.

Nina opened the car door and slid under the driving wheel, pulling the door to. I lit a cigarette while I kept a sharp lookout, up and down the street.

She was out again almost at once.

'It's all right,' she said, taking my arm and moving away from the car. 'The ignition isn't locked.'

'We can't do a thing until after one o'clock,' I said. 'We'd better go back.'

'Let's walk. I don't want to sit at home and wait.'

I could understand that, so we walked slowly down to the sea. That part of the beach was deserted. We sat on the sea wall and looked across the bay at the distant lights of Palm City.

'Harry,' Nina said after a while, 'are you sure the girl was murdered? She couldn't have committed suicide?'

'Not a chance. She was strangled. No, she was murdered all right.'

'Who could have done it?'

'I keep asking myself that. Unless it was some maniac who saw her going to the cabin and attacked her, then it's my bet Rhea is responsible. She has the motive.' I went on to tell Nina what Tim Cowley had told me about the hereditary laws of France.

'If Odette had lived, she would have inherited half Malrouies enormous fortune by right. Malroux is a dying man. It's pretty convenient for Rhea that Odette should die like this, but I can't believe she killed the girl herself. I'm willing to bet this alibi of hers — being ill and taking a sedative — will stand up. She's too smart to be caught out in a false alibi. Sooner or later, Renick will get around to the fact. Odette was to inherit half the fortune. If he suspects the kidnapping was faked, this motive will put him on to Rhea, and she's smart enough to know it.'

Nina said, 'This woman, Harry, must have a lover. Don't tell me a woman like her is prepared to live with a sick old man. I've seen her photographs. I'm sure she has a lover.'

She was right, of course. I wondered why I hadn't thought of the possibilities of a lover before.

'Let me think a moment. You've given me an idea.' I lit a

133

cigarette, my mind busy. After a while, I said, 'Let's suppose there is a lover. Rhea tells him, when Malroux dies, half the fortune goes to Odette. Suppose this guy, thinks it would be better for the two of them to grab the lot. Neither of them are willing to take the risk of murdering Odette, so they look around for a fall guy and they pick on me. The kidnap plot is just a smoke screen. I fall for it. Odette falls for it too. Why she falls for it, defeats me, but she falls for it. Rhea and her boy friend are sitting pretty. If anything goes wrong, I'm the guy who'll take the rap. The more I think about it, the more sure I am you're right. There is a man behind all this — the lover and he must be the one who killed Odette.'

For the next hour we talked, speculated and tried to plan, but we didn't get anywhere. All the time, we both were thinking that the minutes were bringing us closer and closer to the time when we had to steal the car and move Odette's body. It was a thought that froze both of us.

Somewhere in the distance, a clock chimed one. Nina looked at me.

'We'd better make a start.'

Neither of us spoke on the way back to the bungalow.

We walked side by side, holding hands. There war nothing to say, both of us realized the full horror to which we were walking.

The street in which we lived was deserted. By now the TV sets had been turned off. The windows of the neat bungalows were dark. We were alone in this little suburban world.

At the intersection of Pacific Avenue and Pacific Boulevard, we paused.

'We'll get the car,' I said.

We walked down Pacific Boulevard until we came to the Mercury. Every house and bungalow was in darkness. Without hesitation, Nina slid into the driving seat and started the engine. I went around to the off-side door which she opened for me and I got in beside her, being careful not to touch any part of the car. She drove the car into our street and pulled up outside our bungalow' I got out to open the gates and then the garage doors. Nina backed the Mercury down the runway. The Mercury and the Packard were now bumper to bumper.

Nina got out of the car and joined me. We both looked at the trunk of the Packard.

This was the moment.

'Go into the bungalow and wait for me,' I said.

'I'll help you, Harry,' she said, a quaver in her voice.

I put my arms around her and hugged her. I knew what it meant for her to make such an offer.

'I'm handling this myself,' I said. 'You must leave me to it.'

'I'll stand by the gate, just in case...'

She walked to the gates and stood there, looking up and down the road.

I went to the garage and took up the tyre lever and forced open the trunk of the Mercury. I swung up the lid.

I then unlocked the trunk of the Packard and swung it open.

The distant clock struck the quarter of the hour.

I dragged Odette's body from the Packard's trunk into the trunk of the Mercury. Handling her was a gruesome experience: an experience I will take to my grave.

While Nina continued to watch, I went into the bungalow and got the briefcase. I put it beside the dead girl and then I closed the lid of the trunk.

'Okay,' I said to Nina. 'Let's go.'

We got in the car. We were close together. I could feel she was trembling. She drove the car to the corner of Pacific Boulevard and there we left it. Silently, we walked back to the bungalow. We met no one.

As I shut the front door, Nina gave a strangled sigh and slid to the floor in a faint.

CHAPTER ELEVEN
I

THEY found Odette's body a little after ten o'clock the following morning..

I had been in my office since nine o'clock, sweating it out and waiting for the telephone bell to ring.

I had had a pretty bad night. When Nina came out of her faint she developed symptoms of shock, and I had had quite a time with her. I finally made her take two sleeping tablets. Once I was satisfied she was asleep, I had gone to the garage and collected Odette's suitcase from the trunk. I had then examined every inch of the trunk to make certain there was no trace of her to be found if those two soldiers came back in the morning to search the car. I even went over the inside of the trunk with the electric cleaner.

Then I took the suitcase to the furnace room and lit the furnace. I opened the case. It contained the scarlet dress she had worn when she had gone to the Pirates' Cabin, the white plastic mack, the red wig and the usual toilet things a girl carries on a journey. I burned the lot, and I cut up the suitcase and burned that too.

I scarcely had any sleep that night and I was feeling pretty bad when I left for the office the following morning. Nina looked ill. We didn't say much to each other. Both of us had this sick feeling of dread, knowing before very long the body must be found.

I found it impossible to work. I sat at my desk with a file in front of me and smoked endless cigarettes, waiting for the telephone bell to ring.

When it did finally ring, my hand was shaking so badly I nearly dropped the receiver.

'We've found her !' Renick's voice sounded excited. 'They have her down at headquarters. Come on, I'm on my way now.

I found him and Barty waiting at the elevators. Barty was pressing the call button impatiently.

'She's dead,' Renick said to me as I came up. 'She's been murdered. She was found in the trunk of a stolen car in Pacific Boulevard.'

136

Little was said on the quick trip to headquarters. We drove straight into the yard. The Mercury stood in the shade with four or five plain clothes men grouped around it, watching a photographer at work.

I felt cold and sick as I got out of the police car and walked with Renick and Barty to the Mercury. I kept my eyes averted as Renick looked into the trunk.

'I want the Medical Examiner to have her as soon as the photographer has finished,' he said to one of the plain clothes men. 'I want you boys to go over every inch of this car. Don't miss a thing.' He squatted down to stare again into the trunk. 'Hey, what's this? Looks like the ransom briefcase.' He took out his handkerchief, reached inside the trunk and covering the handle of the case with the handkerchief he lifted it out. 'Don't tell me the money's here. It's heavy enough.' He set the case down and opened it while the other detectives crowded around. 'Full of newspapers!' he looked at Barty. 'What the hell does this mean?'

'Look at the dress she's wearing,' Barty said. "The barman at the Pirates' Cabin said she had on a red dress and a white plastic mack. She's changed her clothes.'

I had known the risk I was taking with the cheap blue and white dress, but nothing would have induced me to have taken the dress off the body and put the red dress back on her. It was something I couldn't have done.

'Where did the dress come from?' Renick asked, puzzled. He turned to me. 'Look, Harry, take a car and go to Malroux's place. Ask Mrs. Malroux if the girl owned such a dress and bring someone down here to identify her.

I stared at him.

'You mean you want me to see Mrs. Malroux?'

'Sure, sure,' Renick said impatiently, 'and break the news to the old man. Get O'Reilly to come down and identify her. We don't want Malroux to see her. If he wants to come, warn him she isn't a pretty sight, but check on that dress, it's important.'

'Okay,' I said, and glad to get away from the Mercury and its gruesome contents I got into the police car and drove out of the yard.

Now, at last, I had the opportunity to talk to Rhea. Renick

could trace that blue and white dress. Rhea had bought it, She was in for the jolt of her life.

Ten minutes later, I pulled up outside the Malroux residence. I ran up the steps and punched the bell.

The butler opened the door.

'I'm from police headquarters,' I said. 'Mr. Malroux, please.'

The butler stood aside and let me in.

'Mr. Malroux is far from well this morning. He is still in bed. I don't like to disturb him.'

'Mrs. Malroux will do ... it's important.'

'If you will wait, sir...'

He started off down the long passage. I gave him a start, then moving silently, I went after him. He pushed open a glass swing door and stepped out on to the patio where Rhea lay in a lounging chair. She had on a pale blue shirt and white slacks. She looked extremely cool and beautiful, lying there in the sun. She was reading the newspaper and she glanced up as the butler approached her.

I wasn't giving him a chance to warn her. I stepped out on to the patio.

Rhea saw me. She stiffened. Her eyelids narrowed for a moment, then her expression became completely poker faced.

'Who is this?' she said to the butler.

As she turned, I walked up to her.

'I'm from police headquarters,' I said. 'I'm sorry to disturb you, but it is important.'

Rhea dismissed the butler with a wave of her hand. Neither of us spoke until the glass door had swung behind him, then I pulled up a chair and sat down.

'Hello,' I said. 'Remember me?'

She leaned back, reached for a cigarette and lit it. Her hands were very steady.

'Should I remember you?' she said, lifting her eyebrows. 'What do you want?'

'They have found her,' I said, 'but not in the cabin where you intended them to find her. They found her in a trunk of a stolen car.'

She flicked ash on to the crazy paving.

'Oh? Is she dead?'

138

'You know damn well she's dead!'

'Did you two quarrel over the money? You needn't have murdered her, Mr. Barber.'

Her brazen attitude rattled me.

'You're not getting away with that,' I said. 'You're responsible for her death and you know it!'

'Am I?' Again she lifted her eyebrows. 'I can't imagine anyone but you believing that.'

'Don't kid yourself. You have the motive. When your husband dies, half his fortune was to have gone to Odette. It's much more convenient for all the fortune to come to you, isn't it?'

'Of course.' She smiled. 'But you happen to be the one who planned the kidnapping. You happen to be the one who was to meet her at the cabin. I was in bed when she, died and I can prove it. Where were you?'

'If they catch me, they'll also catch you,' I said.

'Will they? I should have thought it would be your word against mine. I can't imagine the police believing an ex-jailbird.'

'That's right, only I happen to have realized that from the start. I took precautions. I planted a tape recorder in the cabin. I have the whole kidnap plot on tape. Don't kid yourself you can't be pulled into this mess, because you can.'

She became very still. Her glittering eyes stared at me.

'A tape recorder?'

'That's right. Everything we planned is on tape. You have the motive. They may send me to the gas chamber, but at least you'll get twenty years.'

That really jolted her. For a moment her poker face mask slipped. Her hands turned into fists, the colour drained out of her face. She looked suddenly older and very vicious.

'You're lying!'

'Think so? If I get caught you'll get caught too. You just didn't play it smart enough. Now you'd better start praying I don't get caught.'

She recovered her self control. The expressionless mask slipped into place.

'So you're not quite the fool I imagined you to be, Mr. Barber. Well, we'll see how it works out.'

139

'Yeah: we'll see.'

The glass door swung open and I looked around. A tall, heavily built man, wearing a smart chauffeur's uniform, stood in the doorway. This would be the ex-cop, O'Reilly. I was aware he was looking curiously at me. I was surprised to see he was about my age. His sand coloured hair was close cropped. His heavy flashy face was coarsely handsome, and his steady grey eyes had that quizzing penetrating stare that most cops have.

'The car's ready, Madam,' he said.

'I won't be going out this morning,' Rhea said and she got up. 'Mr. Malroux isn't at all well.'

She started across the patio.

'Mrs. Malroux. . .' I said.

She paused and looked at me.

'When Miss Malroux's body was found, she was wearing a blue and white cotton dress. It was quite a cheap thing. Lieutenant Renick is wondering where it came from. You will remember she wore a red dress when she left here. Lieutenant Renick wants to know if you know anything about the dress.'

I thought I would have jolted her with this, but her expression didn't change.

'I know all about the dress,' she said. 'I bought it for her. It is a beach dress. She kept it in her car. When she went to the beach, she changed into it. Perhaps you will tell the Lieutenant that.'

She turned and walked to the glass door which O'Reilly held open for her.

I felt a sudden sinking feeling of uneasiness' If she could be so calm and quick witted on a question like that, could she talk herself out of the tape recording? She could admit the kidnap plot, but that still didn't implicate her in Odette's murder.

'You're Barber, aren't you?' O'Reilly said, and his voice jerked me alert. 'The Lieutenant told me about you. Have they found her?'

Watch it, I thought. This guy is an ex-cop. He has been trained to spot anything suspicious, and what he spots will go straight back to Renick.

'They found her. Renick wants you to come down and identify her.'

O'Reilly grimaced.

'Maybe the old man should do it.'

'She's been dead two days and shut in the trunk of a car. Renick thinks Malroux shouldn't see her.'

'Well, okay.' His grey eyes shifted over my face. 'Have they found the ransom yet?'

'No.'

'I told the Lieutenant: find the ransom and you'll find the killer: it's that simple.'

'They're waiting. Let's go.'

'I'd better tell the old man where I'm going,' he said. 'I won't be a minute.' He started across the patio, then abruptly paused to look at me. 'They've got no clue to the guy who strangled her? That photograph in the paper last night didn't pay off ?

That jolted me. I had forgotten the photograph.

'No.'

'The Lieutenant is smart. He'll bust this case. I've worked with him in the past. He knows his business.'

I watched him go, then I took out my cigarettes. I was about to light one when I had a sudden cold, spooky feeling.

They've got no clue to the guy who strangled her?

I had said nothing about how Odette had been murdered neither to Rhea nor to O'Reilly. 'Her body had only just been discovered. Not even the newspaper men were in on it yet — then how did O'Reilly know she had been strangled?

The cigarette slipped out of my fingers.

Here was my man! The lover! The ex-cop who had Renick's confidence, who had the opportunity of knowing all what was going on and of living in this house within a few yards of Rhea's bedroom.

O'Reilly!

How else could he know Odette had been strangled unless he had strangled her himself?

II

Five or six minutes later, O'Reilly came through the swing doors and joined me on the patio.

141

During those minutes I had got over the shock of my discovery. I had had time to consider more fully the likelihood that he was Odette's killer. He seemed fitted for the job. I told myself I would have to be careful not to give him any idea that I had spotted his slip and was suspicious of him. By now, Rhea would have warned him that I had the tapes. This should jolt him as much as it had jolted her, but it didn't incriminate him. Somehow I had to pin Odette's murder on him before the police pinned it on me.

As he came towards me, silently and smoothly, the way a boxer moves, I had to make an effort to keep my face expressionless.

'All set?'

'Yeah.'

He gave no sign that he knew I had the tapes. His hard fleshy face was a little thoughtful, but that was all.

We went together out of the house and down to the police car.

'Has Mr. Malroux been told?' I asked as I slid under the driving wheel.

'Yeah.' He settled himself in beside me. 'Tough on him his only daughter.'

'Mrs. Malroux took it in her stride,' I said as I drove down the carriageway. 'Did she and the girl get along together?'

'They got along fine,' O'Reilly said, his voice sharpening a little. 'She's not the demonstrative type.' I decided to stick the knife in hard and turn it.

'The Lieutenant was saying Mrs. Malroux now comes into all her husband's money. The girl's death is pretty convenient for her. The girl would have collected half Malroux's fortune if she had lived: now the wife grabs the lot.'

He shifted his solid, muscular body. I didn't risk looking at him.

'There was enough for the two of them, I guess,' he said. I couldn't be sure but I had an idea there was a sudden uneasy note in his voice.

'Some women are never content with the half of anything. Mrs. Malroux strikes me as the type who wouldn't share a breath of air with anyone.'

I felt him stare at me. I didn't look his way.

'The Lieutenant thinks that?'

'I haven't asked him.'

There was a pause, then he said, 'That was a smart idea of his to print that photograph. The guy in the photograph looked a lot like you.'

That counter-attack didn't faz me.

'It was me,' I said. 'We had a description of a man who was seen with the girl at the Pirates' Cabin. His build matched mine. I volunteered to act as a model.' That held him.

'Come to think of it,' I went on, 'you're the same build too.'

He didn't say anything to that one.

We drove two blocks in silence, then I said, 'They found the briefcase. It was in the stolen car with the body.'

His big, powerful hand was lying on his knee. I saw it give a little jump.

'You mean they recovered the ransom?'

'I didn't say that: they have found the briefcase: it was full of old newspapers. Did you know there were two briefcases — exactly alike?'

Again I felt him look at me.

'Yeah.'

'Know what I think? I think someone switched the cases before Malroux left to deliver the ransom. It could easily have been done.'

That really hit him. He dropped his cigarette.

'What are you getting at? Who would switch the cases?' There was a sudden harsh note in his voice. He bent and recovered the cigarette, then tossed it out of the window.

'It's just a theory of mine. The way I figure it is this: the girl gets kidnapped. The old man gets the ransom money ready. His wife suddenly gets a bright idea. If the kidnappers are double crossed, the girl will be murdered.

With the girl out of the way, Mrs. Malroux collects the whole of the estate — not just half of it. So she puts a bundle of newspapers in the other briefcase and switches the cases just before Malroux leaves to deliver the ransom. She then has five hundred grand spending money, she has got rid of her

143

stepdaughter, and when the old man dies, she collects all the millions.'

· He sat absolutely motionless for some moments before in a hard, tight voice, 'Did the Lieutenant think anything of that?'

'I haven't told him yet. It's just a theory of mine.' 'Yeah?' He shifted around in his seat to glare at me. 'Look, take my tip and don't let your imagination run away with you. These folks have plenty of influence. You start a rumour like that, without proof and you'll land yourself in plenty of trouble.'

'I know that,' I said. 'I was just coasting. How do you like the idea yourself?'

'It stinks,' he said, a savage note in his voice. 'Mrs. Malroux would never do such a thing.'

'Is that right? Well, I'll take your word for it. You know her better than I do.'

I swung the car into the police yard before he could come back on that. I pulled up and got out.

We walked together to the morgue. I stood aside to let him go in first.

Renick and Barty were sitting on one of the tables, talking together. Away in a corner on another table was a sheet-covered body.

O'Reilly shook hands with Renick and nodded to Barty.

'So you found her,' he said.

I was watching him. He was as unmoved and as tough-looking as any cop could be.

I watched him cross the room with Renick, then I turned away as Renick flicked back the sheet. I was sweating again.

I heard Renick say, 'Is that her?'

'Sure is — poor kid. So she was strangled. Any angles yet, Lieutenant?'

'Not yet. How did the old man take the news?' 'He's pretty bad.' O'Reilly shook his head. 'The doctor's with him now.'

'Tough.'

They came back to where Barty and I were standing.

'Okay, O'Reilly,' Renick said. 'Thanks for coming. I don't need to keep you. I've got to get on.'

'Anything to oblige Lieutenant,' O'Reilly said. He shook hands, nodded to Barty, gave me a hard stare and went out.

144

Renick said to a plain clothes man who was lounging against the wall:

'Tell the doc he can have her now.'

Jerking his head at me, he left the morgue and crossed the yard. Barty and I followed him.

'What did she say about the dress, Harry?' Renick asked as we all went down the long corridor to the office that had been put at Renick's disposal.

'She knew about it. She bought it herself. It's a beach dress the girl kept in her car. When she went down on the beach she put it on to save a better dress she happened to be wearing.'

Renick pushed open the door to the office and we crowded in.

'I wonder why she changed,' he said thoughtfully. 'Something there that doesn't add up.' He sat down behind the desk and put up his feet.

Barty and I found chairs.

'Why was that briefcase full of newspapers?' Barty asked. 'That puzzles me.'

'And where's the ransom?' Renick picked up a letter opener and started to dig holes in the blotter. 'You know I keep coming back to the idea she was kidnapped someone who knew her. The fact this guy used Jerry Williams's name points to it. We'd better check all her men friends and find out what they were doing at the time she was at the Pirates' Cabin. Will you see to that?'

Barty got to his feet.

'Right away.'

When he had gone, Renick said to me, 'As soon as the doc is through, we'll get that dress photographed. Someone may have noticed her wearing it.'

There came a tap on the door and a police officer looked in.

'There's a guy out here, waiting to see you he said. 'His name is Chris Keller. It's to do with the photograph in the newspaper this morning.'

'Shoot him in,' Renick said, removing his feet from the desk.

I was immediately alert and worried. I looked towards the
door as a man of about my build came in. He paused to look
from Renick to me. I watched his reaction as he and I
exchanged glances, but there was no sign of recognition. I had
never seen him before, and I relaxed.

'Mr. Keller?' Renick said, getting to his feet. He held out
his hand.

'That's right.' Keller shook hands. 'Lieutenant, I saw this
picture in the paper.' He held up the newspaper containing the
picture of myself with the blocked out face...' I think I've seen
this guy.'

'Sit down. Let's have your address, Mr. Keller.'

Keller sat down. He took out his handkerchief and wiped
his sun-tanned, pleasantly ugly face. He said he lived on
Western Avenue and gave the number of his apartment.

'Where do you think you saw this man?'

'At the airport.'

My heart started to thump. I picked up a pencil and began
to doodle on the blotter lying on the desk at which I was I
sitting.

'When was this?'

'Saturday night.'

I saw Renick begin to show interest.

'What time?'

'Around eleven o'clock.'

'What makes you so sure he is the man we're looking for,
Mr. Keller?'

Keller moved uneasily.

'I'm not sure he is the man, Lieutenant It was the suit that
caught my attention. You see I planned to buy a suit like that
myself. I was in the airport lobby waiting for a friend of mine
off the L.A. plane and I saw this guy come in. The suit
attracted my attention. I thought how well it looked, then seeing
this photograph in the paper today, I thought maybe I should
come in and tell you.'

'You did right. Would you recognize this guy again?'

Keller shook his head.

'To tell the honest truth, Lieutenant, I didn't look at his
face. I was looking at the suit.'

146

Renick drew in a long, slow breath of exasperation. Then he asked the question I had been silently willing him not to ask.

'Was he alone?'

'He had a girl with him.'

Renick got slowly to his feet. He could scarcely control his excitement.

'Did you happen to notice the girl, Mr. Keller?' Keller grinned widely.

'Oh, sure. There aren't many pretty girl that I don't notice.'

'How was she dressed?'

'She had on a blue and white cotton dress. She wore big sun goggles and she had red hair — my favourite colouring for a girl.'

'Red hair?' Renick paused in his pacing to stare at Keller. 'You sure about that?'

'I'm sure.'

I took out my handkerchief and surreptitiously wiped my face.

Renick snatched up the telephone.

'Taylor, get that dress the girl was wearing up here right away.'

As he replaced the receiver, Keller said in a puzzled voice, 'I thought you were interested in the guy, Lieutenant, not the girl.'

'What did these two do?' Renick asked, ignoring Keller's remark.

Seeing the hard, seriousness in his eyes, Keller stiffened to attention.

'They came into the lobby. The man was carrying a suitcase. The girl got her ticket checked and the man handed over the suitcase. Then he went away and the girl went through the barrier.'

'Did they speak at all to each other?' Keller shook his head.

'Come to think of it, I don't think they did. The guy just handed over the suitcase and left.'

A police officer came in carrying a blue and white dress. Renick took it from him and held it up so Keller could see it.

'That's the one,' Keller said confidently. 'She looked real cute in it.'

'You're sure?'

'That's the one, Lieutenant.'

'Okay, Mr. Keller. I'll be seeing you again. Thanks for your help,' and nodding to the police officer to take Keller out, Renick went to the telephone and called Barty to come in.

I felt as if a noose was slowly tightening around my throat. I just sat there, doodling and sweating.

'There's something phoney about this business,' Renick said, sitting down at his desk. 'I've had an idea from the very start that this wasn't a straightforward kidnapping.'

'What do you mean?' I said, aware my voice sounded husky.

'I damned if I know, but I'm going to find out.' Barty came in.

'What's up?'

Renick told him what Keller had said.

Barty sat on the edge of the desk, frowning.

'She went alone, but a redhead. This girl's dark. There's two of them - Keller and the air hostess who both swear the girl was a redhead. What was she listed as on the flight - record?'

Renick took out a file and glanced through it.

'Ann Harcourt: booked for L.A. Who's Ann Harcourt? Look, Barty, drop everything. I want to know everything about this girl. Get the boys working. Get L.A. to check on her there. I want all the hotels checked just in case she stayed at a hotel.'

'Just what's on your mind, John?'

'There's something phoney about this set-up. The kidnapper tells the girl he is Jerry Williams who she hasn't seen for a couple of months. He persuades her to go to a joint like the Pirates' Cabin: a place where none of these youngsters ever go. From there she suddenly vanishes. A big guy wearing a brown sports suit is seen in her car at ten-thirty. Another car is heard to drive off, but is not seen. Then a big guy in a brown sports suit is seen with a girl wearing the same dress the murdered girl is found in at the airport at eleven o'clock. That would make the timing right. From the Pirate Cabin to the airport is just about half an hour's drive. So far so good. She could have been kidnapped. She could have been so terrorized that she changed her dress, put on a red wig and sun goggles and gone with the man. But what happens?' He slammed his fist down on the desk. *'She goes alone!* There were fourteen other people travelling in the plane, all in couples. They couldn't have had anything to do with this girl. The air hostess knows them all! This man who was driving her car, walks out of the airport and disappears. Then the briefcase containing the ransom money is found with the murdered girl. It's staffed full of old newspapers, and a rather sinister fact comes out there are two briefcases, the replica of each other.' He paused to stare at Barty. 'Make anything of it so far?'

"Could have been a faked kidnapping,' Barty said. 'Providing this girl Ann Harcourt was Odette Malroux. That's something we'll have to find out.'

'Yeah,' Renick said. 'Okay, get going. Let's check on this girl, and when I say check, I mean check!'

He swung round to me.

'Get that dress photographed. Get one of the office girls to put it on and block out her face. Someone else might recognize it. Get the picture circulated in all the local papers and in L.A.'

I picked up the dress and went back to my office. I felt as if I hadn't a bone in my body. The teeth of the trap were closing too fast. In another twenty-four hours, if not sooner, Renick might even be on to me. Somehow I had to think of a way to prove that O'Reilly had killed her — but how?

I was too busy for the next hour to think about my problem. I got the dress photographed, gave a Press meeting and made sure the photograph would be circulated in Los Angeles.

By then it was lunch time. I was preparing to go to lunch with Renick and Barty when the telephone bell rang. We three were in Renick's office. He answered the phone, then handed the receiver to me.

'It's Nina,' he said. 'She wants you.'

I took the receiver.

'Yes?' I said. 'I'm just going to lunch.'

149

'Harry, will you please come home?' There was a note in her voice — a note I had never heard before — that sent a chill shaking up my spine. 'I have to talk to you.' The fear, the cold flat tone in her voice shook me.

'I'll be right over,' I said and hung up. 'Nina wants me to have lunch with her. Something's come up. One of the usual domestic things,' I said. 'I'll be back by two o'clock.'

'Sure, go ahead,' Renick said. He was reading a file and didn't even look up. 'Take a car, Harry. I want you back here at two o'clock.'

As soon as I left his office, I ran down the passage and down the stairs. I got in a police car and drove home fast. I knew something had happened. I couldn't imagine what but I knew from the tone of her voice it was bad.

I parked the car outside the bungalow and walked fast up the path, took out my key and pushed open the front door.

'Nina?'

'I'm here, Harry,' she said from the lounge.

I crossed the hall, pushed open the lounge door and entered. Then I stopped short.

Nina sat in a chair, facing me. She looked small and scared and very white.

Seated near her, his legs crossed was O'Reilly. He had changed out of his chauffeur's uniform and he had on a sports shirt and bottle green slacks. He was picking his teeth with a match splinter and he grinned at me as our eyes met.

In his right hand, he held a .38 police automatic. Its blunt blue nose was pointing at me.

CHAPTER TWELVE

I

'Come on in, buster, and join the party,' O'Reilly said.

'Your wife doesn't seem to appreciate my company.'

I moved into the room and over to Nina. I was quickly over the shock of finding this man in my home, and a cold fury was taking the place of my first pang of fear.

'You'd better get out before I throw you out,' I said.

He grinned, showing even white teeth.

'Look, buster,' he said, 'you may be a good guy in your own class, but you're not in my class. I could take two like you and think nothing of it.'

Nina put her hand on my arm. Her fingers telegraphed a warning for caution.

'What do you want?' I demanded.

'What do you think? Those tapes and I'm going to have them!'

'So you did kill her!'

He rubbed the side of his jaw as his grin widened.

'Did I? The evidence shows you are the guy who did it. Brother! What a sucker you are! You talk too much. If you had kept your trap shut about those tapes, Rhea and me would have imagined we were sitting pretty, but you had to sound off. Those tapes put Rhea out on a limb. They don't bother me, but she and I are working together on this thing, so I promised her I'd get the tapes.'

'Too bad,' I said. 'You're not getting them. If anyone gets them it'll be Renick.'

He glanced at the gun in his hand and then at me.

'Suppose I aim this rod at your wife's left leg,' he said. 'Suppose I pull the trigger? I could do it if you don't hand over the tapes.'

Nina said quietly, 'Don't listen to him. Harry. I'm not frightened of him.'

I said, 'You fire that gun, and we'll have at least ten people at the door before you can get away. That kind of cheap bluff won't work. Now get out!'

He leaned back in his chair and laughed.

Well, it was worth a try,' he said. 'You're right. I wouldn't shoot either of you.' He slid the gun into his hip pocket. 'Okay, let's get down to business. I want the tapes and you're going to hand them over to me. Where are they?'

'In my bank where you can't get them.'

'Come on, sucker. We'll go to the bank and you'll hand them over. Let's go.'

'You're not having them! That's final. Now get out!'

151

He stared at me for a long moment.

'Well, okay, if that's the way it has to be,' he said, not moving. 'Now I'll convince you you're going to part with them. There are millions of dollars involved in this thing. Those tapes could unstick a plan I've really worked at, and that's not going to happen. I don't give a damn what happens so long as this plan of mine sticks. I have all the money I need to back up the right kind of action to get the tapes. Now, I'll show you something.' He took from his pocket a small bottle of blue glass. He removed the cork and very gently poured liquid from the bottle on to the occasional table at his side. The liquid seemed alive. It hissed as it made a tiny puddle in the middle of the table. I could see it stripping off the varnish and stain. 'This is sulphuric acid,' he went on. 'It's the stuff you throw in people's faces who don't co-operate.' His expression suddenly turned vicious as he stared at me. 'I know a mob who would arrange to throw this stuff at your wife, Barber, for less than a hundred bucks. They are a tough mob. Don't kid yourself you could protect her. They would bust in here when you weren't expecting them and give it to her and take care of you. I either get the tapes right now or within twelve hours your wife will be blind and her flesh will be burned off her face. What's it to be?'

I felt Nina's fingers gripping my arm. We both stared at the bubbling, hissing liquid on the table. I looked at O'Reilly. The expression in those small grey eyes convinced me he wasn't bluffing. He would do this thing. It wasn't possible for me to protect Nina.

I was licked, and I knew it.

I stood up.'

'Okay, let's go.'

Nina caught hold of my arm.

'No! You're not to! He wouldn't dare do it! Harry, please...'

I shook her off.

'This is my mess — not yours.'

I went to the door while she sat motionless, wide-eyed, staring at me.

O'Reilly got to his feet.

'He's right, baby. You keep quiet. Watch out how you clear up that mess. You don't want to burn your pretty hands.'

'Harry!' Nina exclaimed, jumping up. 'Don't do it!'
Don't let him have them!'

I went out of the bungalow and down to the car with
O'Reilly following me. He got in the car beside me.

'Tough luck, sucker,' he said, 'but you should keep your
trap shut. Now you're right on your own. How's Renick getting
on? Hasn't he got on to you yet?'

'Not yet.' I pulled away from the kerb. I hated this man
with a cold vicious fury that almost stifled me. I realized too late
how stupid I had been to have taunted Rhea with the threat
of the tapes. Once I had parted with them, as O'Reilly had said,
I was on my own. It would be my word against hers, and she
could afford to hire the best attorney in the country to make
mincemeat of my story.

'When you're picked up, sucker,' O'Reilly said, 'don't try to
involve Rhea nor me. We both have cast iron alibis.'

'That's nice for you, I said.

We looked at each other. There was a puzzled expression
in his eyes.

'You're a pretty cool punk considering the jam you're in,'
he said. 'I didn't think you had so much nerve.'

'I walked into this mess,' I said, 'and I'm prepared to take
what is coming to me. Everything looks perfect right now, but
you're going to come unstuck because you don't know a damn
thing about women.

That hit him. He twisted around to stare at me.

'What the hell do you mean.

'You'll find out. I've been a newspaper man for years' I've
had plenty of experience with show girls. I know their mentality.
This I do know: Rhea Malroux isn't planning to spend the rest
of her days with an Irish roughneck. You're not kidding yourself
you're anything better than a Irish ex-cop with as much polish
as a sheet of sandpaper, are you? When Malroux dies and she
comes into the money, she'll suddenly lase interest in you. You'll
find you'll be eased out. She'll know how to do it. You Won't
realize what's happening until you are just another ex-cop in
search of another job.'

'Yeah? Is that what you think?' his thin lips moved into
a grin, but there was no grin in his eyes. 'Don't kid yourself,

153

sucker. Long after you have ceased to exist me and Rhea'll be married.'

I managed to laugh.

'That's about the funniest thing I've ever heard.' I swung the car to the kerb outside my bank. The time was now three minutes to two. The bank doors were still shut. You really imagine a woman like Rhea would marry an Irish roughneck like you? Well, maybe I'm a sucker, but I'm not the only one.'

'You shut your trap unless you want me to shut it for you,' he snarled his flesh face turning red.

'Sure. I won't say another word if you're that sensitive,' I said, paused then went on, 'But I know what I'd do if I was in the fix you're in.'

He eyed me.

'Yeah? So what would you do?'

I felt a quickening of excitement. I had got him going. I felt it.

'I'd make damn sure Rhea couldn't throw me out. I'd make sure I was the boss from now on. . .'

He sat motionless. I could almost hear his brain creak as he thought, then suddenly he smiled.

'I'm sorry for you, punk,' he said. 'You're so stupid it isn't true.'

'Okay,' I said, 'so I'm stupid.'

A clerk opened the bank doors.

'But I'll tell you something,' I went on. 'Don't bet on anything from now on. I'll fix you if I can. Rhea will fix you for sure. You'll be a bigger sucker than I am, but I won't be sorry for you.'

He got out of the car. 'Come on, punk. Give your mouth a rest. I want those tapes.'

We went into the bank and I got the tapes. I gave them to him — there was nothing else I could do.

'Don't lose them,' I said as he took the two packets. They are now as important to you as they were to me.'

'You don't have to tell me a thing,' he said and walked out of the bank, a worried, tense expression on his fleshy handsome face.

II

I got back to my office at ten minutes after two. There was a note on my desk, saying Renick wanted to see me as soon as I got back.

This could mean anything – more discoveries – anything. It could even mean he knew now I was the man in the brown sports suit. But I was beyond caring. I had taken my beating and I was now punch drunk. I knew once Renick caught up with me I was cooked. I had no recorded evidence to support my story. Odette's murder could be pinned on me without the slightest trouble.

If I were going to save myself I had to prove somehow that O'Reilly had murdered Odette. I felt pretty sure I had planted the seed of doubt in his mind that Rhea wasn't to, be trusted. He wasn't likely to destroy those two tapes: they represented his only hold on her. So long as they remained in existence, I still had a chance of beating this thing.

I knew Nina must be waiting anxiously for news so I telephoned her.

We were using a line that went straight through the switchboard so I was careful what I said.

'He's got them,' I said. 'There was no other way. Don't say anything. Let me do the talking. It's not as bad as it could be. We'll talk about it when I come back. As soon as I can get away from here, I'll be right back.'

'All right, Harry.'

The shake in her voice made me feel bad.

'Don't worry, darling. I'll fix it somehow,' and I hung up.

It was twenty minutes after two when I pushed open Renick's door and walked into his office.

He was reading a report, a frown of concentration on his lean face. He glanced up as I came in and waved me to a chair.

'I won't be a second,' he said.

Maybe my imagination was playing me tricks, but I had the immediate impression from the tone of his voice that we weren't on the same friendly footing as we had been not an hour and a half ago.

I sat down and lit a cigarette. I had got beyond fear. I was

155

not fatalistic. I was going to bluff this thing to the end, and if my bluff didn't work I'd take what was coming to me.

Finally, he dropped the report on the desk and leaned back in his chair while he looked fixedly at me. His face was expressionless but his eyes were probing. He was now looking at me the way a policeman looks at a suspect — or was I imagining it?

'Harry, have you ever met and talked with Odette Malroux?' he asked.

My heart skipped a beat.

'No. The family came here when I was in jail. I never got the chance of interviewing her,' I said, deliberately misunderstanding him. I thought: the first lie. I would have to go on lying from now on until Renick caught me out in one.

'So you don't know a thing about her?'

'Not a thing.' I flicked ash into the ash-tray. 'Why do you ask, John?'

'I just wondered. I'm hunting for every scrap of information.'

'Maybe there is one thing that might help. Malroux is a French national. The hereditary system in France is so fixed that a child can't be disinherited. Odette would have come into half Malroux's fortune by right if she had survived him. Now she is dead, his wife gets the lot.'

'That's interesting.'

I had the impression that this wasn't news to him. He had known this before I told him. There was a pause, then he said, 'You wouldn't know if the girl had a lover. She wasn't a virgin.'

'I don't know a thing about her, John,' I said steadily

The door jerked open and Barty came in.

'I've got something for you, John,' he said, ignoring me. 'The L.A. police have hit the jackpot. Practically the first hotel they called on jelled. A girl, calling herself Ann Harcourt, booked in at the Regent Hotel. It's a quiet, respectable hotel with no record for trouble. The clerk described her. She was wearing the blue and white dress. She arrived at the hotel at half past midnight by taxi. They have traced the taxi and the driver remembers picking her up at the airport. The only plane in at that time was from Palm City. The girl stayed in her room all

Sunday and had her meals sent up. She said she wasn't well. She had a long distance telephone call from Palm City around nine o'clock in the evening. She remained in her room all Monday, then checked out at ten o'clock in the evening, taking a taxi from the rank. The driver says he drove her to the airport.'

'Did she leave any fingerprints in the hotel room?'

'She did better than that. She left a cheap plastic hairbrush which the maid saw her using. They have a beautiful set of prints from it and the prints are on the wire now. We'll have them any minute.'

'It's my bet,' Renick said, 'Ann Harcourt was Odette Malroux.' He picked up the report he was reading. 'Just got the autopsy report. She was hit on the back of the head and stunned, then she was strangled. There was no struggle. She was taken by surprise. Here's one thing that's interesting, Barty. Between her toes and in her shoes was sand — beach sand. It looks as if she had gone to the beach and walked along the sands to a rendezvous. The lab boys think they can place the beach where the sand came from.'

Barty grunted.

'They are always thinking they can work miracles.'

It was uncanny and disturbing to sit there, listening to these two men talk and being sharply aware that both of them were ignoring me. I might just as well not have been in the office for all the notice they paid me.

'Well, if you don't want me, John,' I said, getting up, 'I'll get back to my office. I've a whale of a lot of work to do.'

They both turned and stared at me.

'That's okay,' Renick said, 'but don't leave the building. I'll need you in a little while.'

'I'll be in my office.'

I went out and walked down the passage to my office.

Standing at the head of the stairs, the only exit to the street, were a couple of detectives, talking together. They glanced at me casually and then away.

I went into my office and shut the door.

Were these two guarding the stairs? Making sure I wouldn't bolt?

I sat down at my desk aware of a little spark of panic in

157

my mind. Was I already trapped? Had Renick guessed I was involved in this mess?

I tried to work, but concentration was impossible. I paced up and down, smoking cigarettes, trying to think of a way to trap O'Reilly, but I just couldn't think of one.

After an hour, I left the office and went into the washroom. The two detectives still stood at the head of the stairs.

On my return, the telephone bell rang.

'Come in, will you?' Renick said.

My nerves were now really on the jump. If it hadn't been for those two guarding the stairs, I might even have bolted.

I braced myself and walked down the passage to Renick's office. He was just coming out as I arrived.

'Meadows wants us,' he said and leading the way, he went to Meadows's office.

Meadows was at work at his desk. He looked up as we came in.

'Well? What's cooking?' he asked, reaching for a cigar.

'What's it all about, John?'

Renick sat down. I went over to an empty desk away from them and sat down.

'I'm satisfied now, sir, the girl was never kidnapped,' Renick said.

Meadows paused as he was about to bite off the end of his cigar and stared.

'Never kidnapped!'

"It was a faked kidnapping. She and this guy in the sports suit planned it together. It's my guess he was after the money and persuaded her to help him get it. The only possible way to get it from her father was to pretend she had been kidnapped.'

Meadows blew out his cheeks. He looked stunned.

'You'd better be sure about this, John.'

'I"m sure enough,' Renick said, and went on to tell Meadows about the new evidence that had come in about Ann Harcourt. 'We got her fingerprints ten minutes ago. She was Odette Malroux — no mistake about that. We know she went to Los Angeles on her own and came back on her own. That means she did the trip of her own free will. She certainly wasn't kidnapped.'

'Well, I'll be damned!' Meadows muttered. 'How did she get murdered?'

'Her partner collected the ransom and these two agreed to meet somewhere. He probably wanted all the money, so to silence her, he knocked her on the head and strangled her.'

My hands were in fists and my nails dug into my palms as Renick talked.

'Who is he? Have you got a line on him yet?' Meadows asked.

'I have several lines on him,' Renick said quietly, 'but not enough to book him. Doc tells me there was sand in the dead girl's shoes — beach sand. The lab boys are trying to locate where the sand comes from. They think they can do it. It's my bet Odette arranged to meet her killer at one of the beach centres along the coast.'

Meadows got to his feet and began to prowl around his office.

'We'd better not release any of this to the Press, Barber,' he said. 'This could be dynamite.'

'Yes,' I said.

He looked at Renick.

'You really think this girl tried to gyp her father out of five hundred grand?'

'I think the killer talked her into it,' Renick said. 'He was probably her lover. She fell for his talk and then got herself murdered.'

I had to say something I just couldn't sit there like a dummy.

'If he collected the ransom,' I said, hoping my voice was steadier than it sounded, 'why didn't he skip? He didn't have to meet and kill her.'

Renick glanced at me, then away. He lit a cigarette.

'Suppose he had skipped with the money? The girl might have told her father. The killer probably guessed she would be dangerous if he double-crossed her. It was safer to silence her.'

The telephone bell rang.

Renick answered it.

He listened for a moment, then said, 'You have? That's fine. You're sure? Okay,' and he hung up. Turning to Meadows,

159

lie went on, 'The lab boys say the sand in her shoes comes from East Beach. It is an artificial beach there and they are absolutely sure the sand comes from East Beach, and nowhere else. There's a bathing station there with cabins. That's where they must have met. I'll get down there now.' He looked at me. 'You'd better come with me, Harry.'

That's just what I didn't want to do. Bill Holden would recognize me. Then with a sudden prickle of fear, I remembered I hadn't paid lam the last week's rent on the cabin.

'I'd better get on with my work, John. I'm getting way behind,' I said, aware my voice sounded breathless.

'Never mind the routine stuff,' Renick said curtly.

'That can look after itself. I want you with me.'

'And listen, Barber, no more information for the Press,' Meadows said.' Let them know we're still working on the case, of course, but that we've struck a slow patch. Start playing it down. If it gets out this girl faked her own kidnapping to get money for her lover from her father phew! what a stink!'

I said I understood.

While he was talking, Renick was on the telephone, alerting his team.

'Let's go,' he said, hanging up. To Meadows, he went on, 'I'll report to you, sir, as soon as I get back.'

As I walked behind Renick out of the office, I wondered if I could borrow money from him to pay Holden. I decided not to try. I couldn't imagine he would have fifty dollars on him anyway. I just hoped that Holden wouldn't mention that I hadn't paid him. It wasn't much of a hope, but there was nothing I could do about it.

As we reached the head of the stairs, I saw Renick give a quick signal to the two waiting detectives. They followed us down the stairs to where two cars were waiting. Renick and I got in the back of one, the two detectives got in the front with the driver. The car shot away, followed by the second car with the technical men.

We reached East Beach around six o'clock. The beach was still crowded.

Renick told his men to remain in the cars. Nodding to me, he walked to the entrance of the bathing station. I plodded behind him, feeling the way a steer probably feels when going to be slaughtered.

Bill Holden was in his office. He looked up as Renick and I came in.

'Why, hello Mr. Barber,' he said, getting to his feet. He looked inquiringly at Renick.

'This is Lieutenant Renick, City Police, Bill,' I said. 'He wants to ask you a few questions.'

Holden looked startled.

'Why sure, Lieutenant. Go right ahead.'

Here it comes, I thought. This is something, if I can't lie myself out of, that'll sink me.

Renick said, 'We're trying to trace a girl: she's around twenty, pretty, with red hair and wearing a blue and white cotton dress. She wore big sun goggles and ballet type shoes. Mean anything to you?'

Holden didn't hesitate. He shook his head.

'I'm sorry, Lieutenant, it's no good asking me a thing like that. I see thousands of girls here during the season. To me, they're like so many grains of sand. I never even see them.'

'We have reason to believe this girl was here around midnight on Saturday. Were you here Saturday night?'

'No. I went off duty at eight.' Holden looked at me, 'but you were here, weren't you, Mr. Barber?'

Somehow I managed to look a lot calmer than I felt.

'Not Saturday, Bill. I was at home.'

Renick was staring at me.

'Well, then I guess I can't help you, Lieutenant,' Holden said.

'What makes you think Mr. Barber was here on Saturday night?' Renick asled in a deceptively mild voice.

'I just imagined he was. He...'   '

I cut in.

I had rented a cabin here, John. I was planning a book. I found I couldn't work at home.'

'Is — that — right?' The unbelief in his voice was painful to hear. 'You didn't tell me that.'

I forced a grin.

'The book didn't jell.'

161

Renick stared at me for a moment, then turned to Holden. 'Were all the cabins locked on Saturday night?'

'Sure,' Holden said. 'I locked them myself: except Mr. Barber's cabin of course. He had the key.'

'None of the locks had been tampered with?'

'No.'

'Did you lock your cabin, Harry?' Renick asked.

'I think so. I can't be sure. Maybe I didn't.'

'Which was your cabin?'

'The last one on the left, Lieutenant,' Holden said. He was now uneasy and he kept shooting glances at me and then at Renick.

'Anyone in the cabin now?'

Holden looked at a chart on the wall.

'It's empty right now.'

'Have you ever seen Odette Malroux here?' Renick asked.

'The girl who was kidnapped?' Holden shook his head. 'She never came here, Lieutenant. I'd know her. I've seen enough pictures of her. No ... she never came here.' 'I'll take a look at the cabin. Got the key?' 'It'll be in the door, Lieutenant.

Renick started for the door and I started after him.

Holden said, 'Oh Mr. Barber. . .'

Here it comes, I thought. I turned and grimaced at him.

'I'll be right back, I said, and as Renick paused, I crowded up against him, trying to shove him out of the little office.

'What is it?' Renick asked Holden, refusing to be shoved.

'It's okay, Lieutenant,' Holden said, looking unhappy. 'It's nothing important.'

Renick went out into the hot sunshine. We walked in silence along the wooden slats laid on the sand, avoiding the half-naked sun-bathers who stared at us, wondering who we were in our city clothes, until we came to the cabin where Odette had died.

The key was in the lock. Renick pushed open the door and stepped in. He looked around, then turning, he looked hard at me.

'You didn't tell me you had hired this cabin,' Harry?'

'Should I have done?" I remained by the door. 'It didn't cross my mind you'd be interested.'

'This is where she could have been murdered.'

'Think so? She could have been murdered on the beach.'

'I want you to think: did you lock the door or didn't you?'

'I don't have to think — I didn't lock it,' I said. 'I didn't tell Holden that. I didn't want him to get mad at me. I left the key in the lock. I found it on Monday when I looked in to pick up my typewriter.'

'So she could have been murdered here.'

'The locks on these doors don't mean a thing. She could have been murdered in any of the cabins or on the beach.'

He brooded for a long minute while I stood there, listening to the thump-thump-thump of my heartbeats.

Then he glanced at his wrist watch.

'Okay, Harry, you get off home. I don't want you any more for tonight. Get one of the boys to run you home. Tell the others I want them right here.'

'I don't mind sticking around if I can be of any help,' I said.

'It's okay. You get off home.'

He wasn't looking at me now, but staring around the room. I knew what would happen the moment I had gone. They would take the cabin to pieces. The fingerprint boys would test every inch of the place and sooner or later they would find Odette's prints. There was just a chance they would also find Rhea's prints and O'Reilly's prints. They would certainly find mine, but that didn't worry me. What did worry me was that Renick would go back to Bill Holden and ask him if he had seen a big, broad-shouldered man in a brown sports suit, and Holden would tell him I had been wearing a brown sports suit.

But was this proof that I had killed Odette? I didn't think so. I felt I had still a little time: it was running out on me fast, but at least, I had a little time.

'See you tomorrow then, John.'

'That's it.'

He still didn't look at me as I walked out of the cabin and started across the sand to Holden's office.

Holden was standing in the doorway.

'I'm sorry I didn't settle with you, Bill,' I said. 'It went right out of my mind. I'll send you a cheque tomorrow. That okay?'

163

'I'd be glad to have it now, Mr. Barber,' Holden said awkwardly. 'My boss doesn't give credit.'

'I happen to have left my wallet at the office. I'll send you a cheque.'

Before he could argue, I walked on to the waiting police car.

I said to one of the technical men, 'The Lieutenant wants you boys in the cabin at the far end. I'm going home. I'll take the bus.'

One of the detectives who had been guarding the stairs said, 'That's okay, Mr. Barber. We'll run you back. This isn't our pigeon. We've just come for the ride.'

Now was the time to test my suspicions.

'That's okay. I'll take the bus. So long, boys,' and I walked away over to the waiting bus.

As the bus moved off, I looked back over my shoulder.

The two detectives in the police car were right behind the bus.

I knew now for certain the red light was up, and I was suspect Number One for Odette's murder.

CHAPTER THIRTEEN

I

As I stepped into the hall, shutting the front door, Nina came out of the lounge. She was looking pale and anxious. She ran to me, reaching up to kiss me. I put my arms around her, holding her close to me.

'Harry!' She was whispering. 'They have been here this afternoon when I was out, searching the place.' My arms tighted around her.

'What makes you say that?'

'Keep your voice down. Do you you think they have hidden a microphone somewhere?'

I hadn't thought of that possibility. I immediately realized the danger.

'It'll be in the lounge if it is anywhere.'

'I've looked. I can't find it.'

'Wait here.'

I went into the lounge and crossing over to the radio I turned it on, with the volume well up. A second or so later, the room was filled with the strident sound of a jazz session.

I went to the window and looked out. There was no sign of the police car, but I was sure it was there, out of sight, but from where they could watch my front gate. Then I went into the kitchen and looked out of the window. There was an alley running along the bottom of the garden. Two linesmen were working within sight of the kitchen door. One of them was at the top of a telegraph pole: the other lounged at the foot. Neither of them seemed busy.

While Nina watched from the door of the lounge, I made a systematic search for the microphone. I finally found it hidden in the radiator. If I hadn't had some experience of police methods, I would never have found it.

I moved the radio to within a couple of feet of the radiator and let the jazz swamp the microphone.

'They can't hear us now,' I said. 'What made you think they had been here?'

'I don't know — a feeling.' She sat down abruptly, looking at me with frightened eyes. "As soon as I opened the door I felt someone had been here. When I looked in the closet I found my clothes had been disarranged.' She shivered. 'What does it mean, Harry?'

'It means they are on to me. They're watching outside now.'

I had a sudden idea. I went into the bedroom, opened the closet door and checked my suits.

The brown sports suit was missing.

For a long uneasy moment I stood staring at the space where it had hung, then I went back into the lounge.

'They were after my brown suit and they've taken it, I said.

Nina was trying not to cry. It wrung my heart to see her.

'What are we going to do? Oh Harry! I can't bear the thought of losing you again! What will they do to you?'

I knew what they would do to me — they would put me in the gas chamber, but I didn't tell her that.

'Why did you let him have the tapes?' she went on frantically. 'I would rather ...

165

'Stop it! This is my mess! He wasn't bluffing. I had to give them to him!'

She beat her knees with her fists.

'But what are we going to do?'

'I don't know. There must be a way out of this mess. I've been trying to think...'

'You must tell John the whole story. He'll help us. I'm sure he will!'

'He can't do a thing for me. There's no proof. My only possible hope is to make O'Reilly confess, but how do I do that?'

'What happened to the ransom money, Harry?'

I stared at her. A sudden prickle of excitement ran through me. I remembered what O'Reilly had said: *Find the ransom, and you'll find the killer.*

'What is it, Harry? Have you thought of something?'

'The money! Where is it?' I got to my feet and began to pace up and down. 'Five hundred thousand dollars in small bills can't be easily hidden. Where have they hidden it? Not in a bank — that's certain. In the house? Dare they risk that? They must know as soon as I'm arrested, I'll try to incriminate them and Renick will search the house. I can't believe they would risk hiding it there — then where?'

'A safe deposit?'

'It would be risky. They would have to open an account and sign for a key. The most likely place is a left luggage station, either at the airport, the bus station or the railroad station. It would be easy and safe for O'Reilly to check in a suitcase at any of these places. No one would remember him, and he could get the money quickly in an emergency without identifying himself.'

'You must tell John.'

'That wouldn't help me. O'Reilly must be caught getting the suitcase out. He must be caught red-handed to do me any good.'

Nina made a gesture of helplessness.

"But he would never let himself be caught red-handed.'

'That's right. Unless...' I paused, then went on, 'unless I can stampede him by some trick.'

'But how? A manlike that...'

'Let me think about it. Let's have supper. While you're getting it, I'll think. I want to turn the radio off. It's driving me nuts.'

'I'm so frightened. If they took you away.

'It hasn't happened yet. Get hold of yourself, darling. I'm relying on you.'

'Yes, of course.' She got to her feet. I'm sorry, Harry.'

I kissed her.

'Go ahead and let's eat,' I said, then I crossed to the radio and turned it off.

When she had gone into the kitchen, I sat down and really bent my brains to the problem, but it wasn't until we had made a poor meal in silence, that a sudden idea dropped into my mind.

Nina who kept glancing at me expectantly, saw by my sudden change of expression that I had an idea. She began to speak, then remembering the microphone, she stopped. I put the radio on again.

'I think I've got it,' I said. 'There is only one way to work it. I've got to trick him. I think I have an idea how I can do it, but everything depends on whether or not the money is in a left luggage station or a safe deposit. If it's in the house, then I'm sunk, but I can't believe it is in the house.'

'What are you planning to do, Harry?'

'Give me a moment.'

I went to my desk and taking a sheet of paper, I wrote out the following:

NEWS FLASH.

We interrupt this programme to bring to you the latest development in the Malroux kidnapping.

The Palm City police have reason to believe that the ransom money has been lodged in a safe deposit or at a left luggage station.

A special search warrant has been obtained from the State Governor, and beginning at nine o'clock tomorrow morning, teams of detectives are to search all parcels and luggage in left luggage stations and all newly opened safe deposits.

Anyone who has rented a safe since the beginning of the month is asked to call at the nearest police station with the key of the safe.

167

The search will cover a radius of a hundred miles of Palm City. District Attorney Meadows feels confident that, by this extensive operation, the ransom money will be found.

I gave the sheet of paper to Nina who read it. She stared blankly at me.

'I don't understand, Harry.'

'It's my job to feed the local TV and radio stations with news of the kidnapping. They'll broadcast this without question. I'm hoping when O'Reilly hears of this, he'll stampede. He could lead me to the place where he has hidden the money.'

'But you don't know he'll be listening in.'

'He'll be listening in all right. I'm going to tell him to listen in.' I moved to the telephone, then paused. 'They've probably tapped the line by now. I'll have to use an outside line. If it got back to Meadows, he would stop it.' I started for the door. 'I'll go to the drug store at the corner. I'll be right back.'

'Shall I come with you, Harry?'

'Better not. You wait here for me.

By now it was dark. I left the bungalow and strolled down the path to the gate. As I opened the gate, I glanced to the right and left. The police car was parked about fifty yards up the road. The drug store was the other way. I didn't have to pass the car. I set off, walking at a normal pace. I heard the car start up. I knew it was crawling after me but, I didn't look back. My one fear now was that they would arrest me before I could put my plan into operation. If they did that, I was really sunk.

I went into the drug store and shut myself in a booth. I called the local TV station. I got through to Fred Hickson, the P.R.O. and my opposite number.

"Fred,' I said, 'I have an important announcement for you. The D.A. wants it broadcast and put on TV at eleven tonight. Can you do it?'

'Sure: let's have it,' Hickson said.

I read the News Flash to him and he took it down.

'That's okay,' he said. 'We'll interrupt both programmes at eleven o'clock. The D.A. certainly means business, doesn't he?'

'He sure does,' I said. 'Well, thanks, Fred — so long,' and I hung up.

I looked at my watch. It was half past nine. I telephoned Malroux's residence. After a delay, the butler answered.

'This is police headquarters,' I said. 'We want to talk to O'Reilly. Is he there?'

'I believe he is in his room,' the butler said. 'If you will hold on I will connect you.'

There was a clicking on the line, then O'Reilly said, 'Hello! Who is it?'

Speaking slowly and distinctly so he couldn't miss a word, I said, 'Hello, sucker, how's your conscience acting tonight?'

There was a sudden silence. I could imagine him at the other end of the line, his face hardening and his hand tightening on the receiver.

'Who's this?' he demanded, a snarl in his voice.

'The other sucker,' I said.

'Is that you, Barber?'

'Yes. I'm tipping you off. The D.A. has at last come up with a bright idea. If you're interested, and you'd better be interested, listen to the TV programme, local network, at eleven tonight for a news flash. Got it? The local station at eleven tonight. See you in the gas chamber,' and I hung up before he could say anything.

As I came out of the booth I saw a big man with a red face and with cop written all over him come into the store.

I knew sooner or later the axe would fall, but when I saw him my blood ran cold.

He came straight up to me.

'Mr. Barber?'

'That's right.'

'You're wanted at headquarters. We have a car right here.'

'Why sure,' I said, and as we walked together from the store to the waiting car, I thought of Nina.

The detective and I got in the back of the car. The other detective who had been waiting by the car, slid under the driving wheel.

'What's it all about?' I asked as the car shot away. 'Has something come up?'

'I wouldn't know,' the detective said in a bored flat voice. 'They just told me to fetch you, and I'm fetching you.'

There was nothing now I could do. I had played a King and now everything depended on whether O'Reilly held the Ace or only the Queen. If he held the Ace, I was sunk.

II

Renick was working at his desk. The one light in the room came from his green shaded lamp. It made a pool of hard light on his blotter.

The two detectives shepherded me into the office as if they were handling something fragile, then as soon as I was safely delivered, they stepped back into the passage and closed the door.

I walked to a chair and sat down, glad of the heavy shadows in the room.

Renick was smoking. He tossed his pack of cigarettes and his lighter into my lap. There was a sort silence as I lit a cigarette.

'What's up?' I asked as I put the lighter and the cigarettes on the desk. 'I was just going to bed.'

'Let's cut out the bluff, Harry,' he said quietly. 'You're in bad trouble and you must know it.'

'Am I under arrest?'

'Not yet. I thought I'd have a talk with you first. This is off the record. I could lose my job handling it this way, but I've known you, come rain, come sunshine for the past twenty years. You and Nina arc real people to me so I'm giving you a break. I want you to tell me the truth. If you're in the kind of trouble I think you are, I'm handing you over to Reiger. I'm not going to work on you. Let's have the truth and it's strictly off the record: did you kill Odette Malroux?'

I looked at him directly.

'No, but I don't expect you to believe me.'

'There are no microphones in this office, and no witnesses. I'm asking you, not as a police officer, but as your friend.'

'The answer is still the same: I didn't kill her.'

He leaned forward to crush out his cigarette. The white light from the desk lamp lit up his face. He looked as if he hadn't had any sleep for a couple of days.

170

'Well, at least that's something,' he said. 'You're mixed up in this business, aren't you?'

'I certainly am. I'm in such a jam, even having you as a friend ' isn't going to do me any good.'

He lit another cigarette.

'Suppose you tell me the whole story.'

'Sure — how did you get on to me, John?'

'Tim Cowley told me he had seen you at the bus stop on the night of the murder with a redhead, wearing a blue and white dress. I kept checking on you, and everything I turned up pointed to you.'

'I thought maybe Cowley would give me away,' I said wearily. 'I was nuts to have got myself mixed up with these two women, but I wanted the money. They offered me fifty thousand dollars for what looked a pretty simple job. I wanted that money to get out of town and make a fresh start.'

'Let's have the story.'

So I told him. I told him everything except that Nina had helped me move Odette's body. I kept her out of it.

'I thought I was playing safe by having those tapes,' I concluded 'but O'Reilly beat me to it. Now I have nothing — not one thing to support my story.'

All the time I had been talking, Renick had sat motionless, staring at me. Now he drew in a long, slow breath.

'Well — for the love of Mike! What a story!' he exclaimed. 'There's one thing that doesn't seem to add up — how was it Odette co-operated in this kidnapping plan?'

'Yes, that had me guessing, but I've thought about it and it's not all that hard to figure out. It's my guess she fell for O'Reilly. He probably made a terrific play at her. She must have known her father wouldn't let her marry the guy. She wanted money to hold O'Reilly. What she didn't realize was that he had fallen for Rhea. The two of them planned to lead the girl on. One of the two suggested the kidnapping plan — the only possible hope for Odette to lay her hands on a substantial sum of money. She fell for it. The other two used the faked kidnapping to murder her and to make me the fall guy. It could have happened that way.'

'Yes.' Renick brooded for some moments. 'But all this

171

doesn't help you, Harry. We've no proof your story is true. Meadows wouldn't touch it.'

'I know.' I looked at my watch. The time was fifteen minutes after ten. 'This is where you can help me. I've set a trap for O'Reilly. There's a chance he'll lead me to where he's hidden the money. I want you to come With me. It's my one chance of licking this thing. I must have police witnesses.'

Renick hesitated.

'I can't imagine O'Reilly leading you to where he's hidden the ransom. What makes you think he will?'

'It's a gamble, but there's no other way out for me. I'm not going to try to get away, John. I just want your help. If this trick of mine fails, then I'm sunk.'

'Well, all right, but I warn you, Harry I've got to report this and it's my bet Meadows will have you arrested. I've kept it from him up to now, but he's got to be told.'

'Give me an hour. If I can't swing it by then, then I'll take what's coming to me.'

'Well, okay.'

'Can I telephone Nina? She'll be wondering where I am.'

He waved to the telephone.

I called Nina. I told her I was with Renick and said I was going after O'Reilly.

'Keep your fingers crossed for me,' I said, 'and don't worry.' I hung up. To Renick, I said, 'Let's go.' 'Go where?'

'Malroux's place.'

Renick made for the door and I followed him.

The two detectives waiting outside looked inquiringly at Renick.

'I want them along too,' I said.

The four of us walked down to the police car. During the drive out to Malroux's place no one spoke. When we reached the gates, I said, 'We'll walk up. I don't want him to know we're here.'

We reached the house at ten minutes to eleven. The lights were on in three of the ground floor rooms. It was a hot night and all the french windows stood open.

'I'll go first,' I said, 'then you follow on.' Moving silently, I mounted the steps leading to the terrace. Then keeping close to the wall, I walked to the open french windows and cautiously peered in.

They were there'.

O'Reilly in a sports shirt and slacks, was sprawling in a lounging chair, a highball in his hand. Rhea was lying on the settee. She was smoking and she looked far from relaxed.

Renick joined me silently. The two detectives hovered in the shadows behind us.

O'Reilly was saying, 'He's bluffing. You'll see. I bet you it's so much hot air.'

'It's nearly eleven. Turn it on.'

Their voices came clearly to us.

O'Reilly got out of the chair and turned on the big TV set that stood in a corner. He returned to his chair and drank half the highball at a swallow.

There was a gangster film showing. Two men, guns in hand, were stalking each other in the half dark.

Rhea swung her long, slim legs off the settee and stared at the screen. The two of them sat there, waiting.

At eleven o'clock, the picture faded and Fred Hickson appeared on the screen.

'We interrupt this programme to bring you the latest development in the Malroux kidnapping...' he said, and then went on to read the announcement. I had dictated to him. When he had finished, the gangster picture came on again.

I stood there, watching and waiting, so tense I could scarcely breathe. I didn't have to wait long.

O'Reilly jumped to his feet, slopping his drink.

'Goddam it!'

He crossed to the TV set and turned it off, then he spun around, his fleshy face pale, his eyes alarmed.

'Nine o'clock tomorrow! That must mean they haven't the warrant yet or they would have started right away. I'd better get down to the airport!'

I drew in a long breath of relief. My bet had come off. I had guessed right.

'What do you mean?' Rhea demanded.

'Mean?' He scowled at her. 'What do you think I mean? If they find that dough, we'll be in trouble. I'm getting it right

173

away before they find it. I was a dope to have left it there. I might have guessed they would start something like this.'

Rhea got to her feet. Her face was white and her eyes were glittering.

'It's a trap, you fool! Do you imagine Barber would have warned you if he wasn't hoping you'd lead him to where you left the money? He will have told that Lieutenant! They will have detectives waiting for you.'

O'Reilly ran his fingers through his hair.

'Yeah, maybe you've got something there, but we've got to take the risk, baby. Maybe you'd better collect the case. I'll keep out of it.'

'I'm not going. Let them find the money! They can't possibly trace it to us!'

'You'll have to go,' O'Reilly said. I could see his face was glistening with sweat. 'What are you worried about? They wouldn't interfere with you. They wouldn't know you were collecting the dough. They'd think you were just getting a suitcase.'

'I'm not going!' Rhea said, her voice shrill. 'I'm not walking into a stupid trap like that! Let them find the money. There's plenty more where that came from!' O'Reilly moved away from her.

'Look, baby, if you want to save your skin, you'd better go. Those two tapes are with the money.'

Rhea stiffened. 'Tapes? What do you mean?' 'You heard me — those two tapes I got from Barber are with the money.'

'You told me you had destroyed them!'

'Keep your goddam voice down! I didn't destroy them.'

There was a long moment of silence, then she said, 'You're lying!' Her voice was off-key and strident. 'You want that money; You're trying to trick me into getting it for you!'

O'Reilly suddenly looked bored.

'Look, baby, this is your funeral, not mine. I'm telling you — those two tapes are with the money. Okay, I admit it. I've been a mug. I let that cheap shyster Barber talk me into it. He said if I didn't hang on to the tapes you could ditch me, so I went down to the airport and put them with the money. I would have given them to you as a wedding present. Now, you're in trouble. I'm in the clear, but those tapes can fix you. You'd better go down to the airport and get them pronto.'

'You devil!' Rhea said, her voice a vicious whisper. 'You stupid, blundering devil!'

'You're wasting time, baby. If you don't want to spend the rest of your days in jail, you'd better get going.'

'I'm not going! You'll go or I'll tell the police you murdered her! I may go to jail for a few years, but you'll go to the gas chamber. I'll tell them! I'll tell them everything! Do you hear me! I've got your love-letters! I can fix you, you stupid oaf! Now go and get that case!'

'Yeah!' O'Reilly's face suddenly turned to stone. 'So that shyster was right. You would never have married me would you, you bitch? You've never even loved me, have you? I can see it on your face!'

'Marry you?' she screamed at him 'You? I promised you five hundred thousand, didn't I? Do you imagine I'd marry a stupid hick like you? Go and get that money and those tapes!'

A .25 revolver suddenly appeared in his hand. He pointed it at Rhea.

'I've a better idea, baby. How would it be if you decided to put a slug through your head? The cops would accept the suicide theory. They would find the tapes. They would guess you had listened to the broadcast, lost your nerve and took the easy way out, and that would put me in the clear. How do you like that?'

'Put that gun down'!' Rhea said, backing away. 'Barber knows you killed her! He'll tell the police even if I don't.'

O'Reilly grinned viciously.

'He hasn't a prayer. He's no proof. I like my idea better.'

Renick shoved me aside, his hand sliding inside his coat and coming out with a .38. He stepped into the room.

'Drop it!' he shouted.

O'Reilly spun around. The .25 spat fire. It's vicious little bark was half drowned by the bang of the .38.

O'Reilly dropped his gun. He blinked at Renick, then his knees folded and he slid to the floor as Rhea began to scream.

III

O'Reilly lived long enough to sign a statement. It was as I had guessed. Odette had fallen in love with him and had tried to persuade him to go away with her. O'Reilly was already in the toils of Rhea. The kidnapping plot was her idea. He had agreed to murder Odette for the ransom money and providing Rhea found someone to take the rap. So they picked on me.

When the dust finally settled, I found myself in a cell. I had no idea what was going to happen to me, but at least, I did know they couldn't hang the murder on me.

I remained in the cell for two days, then Renick visited me.

'You've got a break, Harry,' he told me. 'Meadows's only hope of nailing this woman is for you to turn State evidence. He is willing to fix it with the judge for you to go free if you'll do it. She's got a battery of attornies who could get her off unless you come in for us. Will you do it?' I didn't hesitate.

'Of course I'll do it.'

'I knew you would. I've seen Nina. She is putting the bungalow in the market. When it's sold, you two had better get out of town and try to make a fresh start some place else.'

'You don't have to tell me,' I said. 'I'll get out fast enough. Can I see Nina?'

'She'll be along this afternoon.'

But why go on?

After a terrific legal battle, Rhea drew fifteen years. If it hadn't been for my evidence she could have beaten this rap. Then I came up before the judge.

He told me what he thought of me. It didn't amount to much but he was wasting time: I didn't think much of myself either. He said he would give me a suspended sentence of five years. If ever I got into any more trouble, the five years would have to be worked off before I began a sentence any other judge might hand out to me. But that was also a waste of time for I was through with trouble.

All I wanted now was Nina and the chance of a fresh start.

Nina was waiting for me as I left court.

She put her hand in mine and smiled at me.

Right at that moment, I felt the fresh start would take care of itself.

THE END

》》 If you've enjoyed this book and would like to discover more great vintage crime and thriller titles, as well as the most exciting crime and thriller authors writing today, visit: 》》

The Murder Room
Where Criminal Minds Meet

themurderroom.com